THE
STRENGTH
OF
Ballerinas

THE
STRENGTH
OF
Ballerinas

NANCY LORENZ

SWEETWATER
BOOKS

An Imprint of Cedar Fort, Inc.
Springville, Utah

ISBN 13: 978-1-4621-1452-8

Published by Sweetwater Books, an imprint of Cedar Fort, Inc.
2373 W. 700 S., Springville, UT 84663
Distributed by Cedar Fort, Inc., www.cedarfort.com

LIBRARY OF CONGRESS CATALOGING-IN-PUBLICATION DATA

Lorenz, Nancy, author.
  The strength of ballerinas / Nancy Lorenz.
  pages cm
  Summary: Sixteen-year-old Kendra's dream of dancing in the Swan Lake ballet, threatened when her family is forced to move across country, looks hopeful when she finds the right new school--until she begins to have dizzy spells and numbness in her legs.
  ISBN 978-1-4621-1452-8 (perfect : alk. paper)
  [1. Ballet dancing--Fiction. 2. Multiple sclerosis--Fiction.] I. Title.
  PZ7.L8845St 2014
  [Fic]--dc23
   2014013391

Cover design by Kristen Reeves
Cover design © 2014 by Lyle Mortimer
Edited and typeset by Melissa J. Caldwell

Printed in the United States of America

10 9 8 7 6 5 4 3 2 1

To my daughter, Gina

Chapter One

Someday I am going to dance like Alyssa Trent.

The thought held steady, transfixed in my mind just as strong as the pointe I held on the worn wooden floorboards. Could I, Kendra Sutton, someday take center stage as a prima? I imagined it as I waited in the corner of the ballet room, but then the image vanished as I remembered my mental notes from this morning—*stretch the jump, maintain lift, and land like a feather.*

"Croisé, present, piqué, piqué, balancé, balancé . . . ," Miss Irina said, clapping the rhythm. "Pas de bourée, glissade, assemblé, glissade, assemblé, développé to first arabesque, en pointe, hold . . . and close fifth . . . Swivel to tendu effacé devant . . . close fifth."

The class rested momentarily, but the teacher continued on and jumped back into the second combination. "Tour

jeté . . . three chassé turns . . . preparation for double pirouette, pas de bourée, arabesque, hold arms . . . and close."
Miss Irina eyed everyone in the room. She was a hawk.

"Excellent, Kendra." I let out the breath I'd been holding, and relief poured through my soul. Miss Irina then
scrutinized my arm positions, my pointe. "Face," she said,
"Look to the side." Miss Irina repositioned my chin, then
walked away. I held my position, waiting for more criticism, but there was none.

Miss Irina circled Liz instead. I knew it was going to
be bad. Miss Irina didn't like my friend Liz. I waited for
the ax to drop.

"You no want apprenticeship?" There it was. Liz went as
pale as the costumes of *Swan Lake*. "Do you?" Miss Irina's
demand made Liz tremble. Tears almost formed in Liz's
eyes, but she fought them back with resolution. Miss Irina
could scare the living daylights out of anyone. "Speak up!"
Miss Irina shouted, and Liz shook her head affirmatively.
"You jump like elephant in circus. Is what you want?" Liz
didn't reply right away. She froze. The other girls in class
stared at Liz, some stifling a laugh at her predicament. I
looked away to give Liz some breathing room, and stared
at the large, familiar ballet room instead. A light dusting
of resin still hung in the air. The large windows of the
practice room let the light of morning stream in, and I
could see the leaves of some trees outside the panes. The
room was deathly quiet now, and time seemed to crawl
as Liz suffered in silence. Everything stopped when Miss
Irina spoke, like a clock stuck at the stroke of midnight.
Even the pianist in the corner sat silently. He looked bored
as he waited an eternity for Miss Irina's next order.

"Speak up!" Miss Irina barked once more.

"No, Miss Irina," Liz mumbled. Though I idolized Miss Irina for her talent, she seemed almost evil.

"And you, Kendra! Lift. You need lift!" Miss Irina moved closer to me again. "And look at your line!" Miss Irina forced my leg into more turn-out. "Stomach in." She hit my abdomen. "Eating cakes this morning?"

"No!" I gasped and my chest heaved. Did I look fat in the mirror? Sweat trickled down the middle of my back. I was out of breath from the moves, but she made me doubt myself even more.

"But combination," Miss Irina continued as she touched my shoulder, "was good." She crooked her mouth into a little smile. "Elizabeth, take a note from Kendra!"

I hated when she pitted Liz against me. She knew we were best friends.

"Work!" Miss Irina turned and called out the next combination.

The combinations grew more and more difficult as the class went on, but I had to be a Spartan. It was preparation for our assessment, which was in a few months, to get into the apprentice program of the ballet company. The Manhattan Dance Company—my mind boggled at the thought of it. Only a handful of girls would make it, and I was driven to be one of them.

I went to stand by Liz as we prepared to perform a combination across the floor. She looked shaken but held back the tears. She hadn't gotten to this level of dance by taking criticism harshly. But that didn't mean she was a total professional just yet.

"Witch!" she whispered brazenly to me, before flashing

a phony smile to Miss Irina and jumping into the next combination. Rolling my eyes, I followed her to the other side of the room.

"Don't worry. As soon as we're in the apprentice program, you won't have to deal with her any more," I muttered, but Liz still frowned.

"Grand fouettés!" Miss Irina clapped her hands again. "You do like Fonteyn . . ." Miss Irina expected the star quality of the 1950's prima with the increased difficulty and slender line of ballet in the 2000s. "Be like Svetlana!"

We also had to be as perfect as Svetlana Zakharova, who had danced with both the Marinsky and the Bolshoi Ballets. We were little Svetlanas in training, with a dose of Margot Fonteyn thrown in. The trouble was that Miss Irina caught every mistake, and she always rubbed it in. The treatment was hard, yes, but she got results. And Miss Irina liked me, for some reason. She said I was her prize pupil, a top contender for the apprenticeship under her tutelage.

Four girls at a time did grand fouettés until they could no longer hold them. One by one they came down and slumped off to the side. My turn came and I began with three other girls, center floor. Round and round we went, and two of the girls dropped out. Liz and I stayed in the running. The fouetté was my best move.

". . . twelve, thirteen . . . ," the girls began to count. "Fourteen, fifteen . . ." Miss Irina continued her clapping and joined in. "Sixteen . . ."

I could tell Liz worked her fouettés for revenge against Miss Irina. She gritted her teeth and spun the fouettés for as long as she could, then fell out.

I was out of breath again, and the sweat poured down my back now, soaking my leotard, but I remembered my Spartan mentality. *Endure.* I went round one more time. *Resist!* I rounded another. "Nineteen," I whispered. *Achieve!* I forced one more grand fouetté out of my body, then ended—not with a slump like the others, but with a pose with extended arms.

"That," Miss Irina stated, "is prima quality. See how Kendra ends with finesse and closure?" Some of the girls grimaced, including nasty Sara Harrington; others heaved a heavy sigh of defeat.

"Dismissed!" Miss Irina exclaimed. "See you tomorrow, darlinks." We all clapped for the end of class, with Liz clapping a little bit harder, just for spite, and then we exited the practice room, making way for the company dancers that crossed us on the way out.

"Miss Irina hates you, I swear!" I threw my arm around Liz's neck for comfort.

"Better get your degree in phys ed while you can." Sara Harrington flung her sweaty pink towel at Liz and laughed as she pranced away. "Soooo gone," she shouted. She laughed all the way down the hall to the dressing room.

"Witch number two." We both laughed at Sara's unnecessary meanness.

"Miss Irina has it in for me. But if I don't make apprentice, my father's going to withdraw his $5,000 annual donation to the Manhattan Dance Company."

"She's hard on you because she knows you can do it." It was partly true. Liz was an excellent dancer, but Miss Irina still enjoyed picking on her.

"I'll know you have it when you do the dance of death,

darlinks," Liz said, imitating Miss Irina. It was spectacularly accurate, and we both giggled.

"I can't wait to dance in the company," I said as I watched the company dancers line up at the barre.

"I can't wait to dance with *him*." Liz stared as Andrei walked by. "Me and Andrei . . ."

"Romance is out of the question," I whispered. "You can never be a perfect dancer if you let love interfere with your art."

"Oh, you're so *Red Shoes*." Liz turned back to the company as they entered the room that we just left.

"No one will interfere with my ballet. And nothing will stop me. Nothing." I grew serious.

"You're obsessed." Liz watched intently as Andrei took off his sweatshirt.

"So are you."

"For a different reason." Liz gasped as Andrei took the barre to warm up.

"Well, I'll take *The Red Shoes* any day. Art before all." I watched along with Liz as the rest of the company entered the dance studio with their flat duck walk. The professional dancers threw their dance bags in the corner and began stretching at the barre. I watched with fascination as the stars of the Manhattan Dance Company's ballet corps readied for class, just like Liz and I had done. On the floor, the company looked almost awkward, just like anybody else. On pointe, however, they became glorious, ethereal spirits.

"We need to correct the adagio," Alyssa Trent commented, and Andrei Voltaskaya walked up behind her. They began the adagio moves and transformed the old wooden practice room into an opulent stage. It was as if they somehow transcended real life. They brought a piece of heaven to us, and we were mere mortals in their presence.

As Liz and I crowded around the door of the practice room with a handful of other students, we watched the professional company interact.

"Look how gorgeous she is," I said, staring at prima Alyssa Trent. "She's my role model."

"Forget her. It's Andrei who's the star." Liz said. For a moment I agreed with her.

I too stared breathlessly as Andrei executed an impromptu pas de deux from *Le Corsaire* with Alyssa. Alyssa went up on pointe in an adagio, and I watched her every move through the open door, mesmerized. Andrei then held the ballerina's waist and she pirouetted perfectly. He held her in arabesque, one way, then another.

"We go over adagio later. I need jumps now," Andrei said, sending us into a tizzy. He improvised tour jetés with cabrioles around the center. Each time he rounded a jump, he stared at us peering in the door jamb of the rehearsal room.

"He knows we're watching," I whispered. Andrei winked as he rounded another jump.

"Oh my gosh!" Liz squealed.

I saw Andrei's golden hair fly in the jump breeze, and it made me realize that I would have to block out any romantic notions of my own. I had to have tunnel vision. A place in the company was my goal. My only goal.

Andrei boldly added a triple pirouette, then another tour de jeté into a too-swift cabriole. It was too fast, I suddenly realized, just as he fell to the floor with a thud. I gasped in horror. The golden boy had fallen. Star Alyssa Trent, however, laughed rather wickedly at him on the wooden floor.

We didn't laugh. Liz and I bolted to give Andrei his dignity before he could see our reaction. The director shooed the other insignificant school dancers away and shut the door to begin the company class inside.

As I walked back to the dressing room with Liz to change, I thought about what I had just seen. It was good to see the famous make mistakes, I thought. Somehow it made me feel that I didn't always have to be so picture-perfect.

Later that night, I stretched on the living room rug and played with my little brother, Petey. It was hard to stretch because I felt bloated from dinner. It was Wednesday night. We always had chicken and noodles on Wednesdays. The casserole was fattening, but once a week I let myself have comfort food. During the rest of the week, I ate sparingly to keep my weight at one hundred pounds. No more, no less. Dad didn't want me to become like one of those anorexics in my ballet class, so we made a compromise. I ate one or two really good meals a week, and he'd continue to pay for my dance training.

Tonight, Dad had acted weird at dinner and twice had dropped noodles on his shirt. I now watched him as he walked through the living room for the fourth time. He ambled into the room, then out again.

Something was up. As I clapped with Petey and stretched on the floor in a right leg split, I studied Dad as he passed by.

"Kendra, I need to talk," Dad said.

I twisted my body a little and changed into a left leg split.

"Okay," I said and stopped the clapping game. My six-year-old brother's hands were tiny and uncoordinated, and sometimes he missed the clap sequence. He wasn't into it anyway, because of his autism.

"I need to talk to you, now."

I drew my legs in and sat cross-legged on the floor. "What?"

Dad had that look on his face that always sent dread through my soul. "Kendra . . ." Dad paused and put his head down. My heart stopped.

"What happened? Did somebody die?"

"We're moving." He blurted the words out as if he might never get to say them if he didn't.

I laughed. "Park Avenue?"

"No," he said, shifting. "California . . ."

For a moment I thought I hadn't heard him right. "What?"

"We're moving to California on Friday."

The shock of his words made me reel. Surely, he was joking. He had to be. But he wasn't. I could see it in his face. Images of *Swan Lake*, Lincoln Center, *The Nutcracker* . . . my career all flew away at hyperspeed pace. My legs started to tremble.

"No way! My whole life is ballet and New York. Are you kidding?" Dad put his hand out to reach me, but I backed away. "You can't do this to me!" I stood up immediately in protest.

"I've been laid off. After twenty years . . ." Dad ran his hand through his salt-and-pepper hair and stared at the wall. He looked as if he had a whopper of a headache.

"My company said they can transfer me to a new location in California. It won't be as much money, though." Dad paused a moment to get his bearings.

"Where will you work?" I couldn't believe it.

"Super Symmetry Computers . . . in Napa Valley."

"Why California?" My voice cracked, but I didn't care.

"It's a job, Kendra. Glad I took that web graphics design course . . ."

I couldn't speak anymore. I was too stunned. My head buzzed with so many images and thoughts. But I had to be strong. My future depended on it. *Strategize!* I thought. *Debate it.*

"Dad!" I said.

"I'm an older worker, Kendra."

"Dad?"

My father sighed. "I have no other choice."

My cool, reasonable manner faded and emotion overpowered me. I wanted to be mature for Dad, but tears defeated my newly found maturity.

"I won't leave! I'll never leave the Manhattan Dance!" A fire engine from the street below startled me as it screamed out its siren and stopped. I ran to the living room window to look down and saw a gurney taken out of the truck. From ten stories up, the firemen and the people gathered on the sidewalk looked like miniatures in a doll house.

I then looked out at the city with tears in my eyes. How could I ever leave Manhattan? As I stared into the night, I remembered Mom and me standing by this very window, watching the lights of the city twinkle. It was the favorite part of our bedtime ritual.

"Jewels," she called the lights. "Like millions of diamonds attached to buildings that sparkle just for us. Make a
wish," she'd say. I'd close my eyes and pray to be a ballerina.

Standing at the window now, I felt a sharp pain tear
into my heart. It had been six years since mom died, and
we'd never again look out on the lights of Manhattan at
the living room window together. Secretly, I kept up the
nightly ritual for both of us, hiding it even from Dad. But
if we moved, I would never get to see those lights or stand
here at the apartment window for Mom ever again . . .
ever again.

The thoughts boomeranged through my head until I
had to bend over and grab my leg. The muscle went stiff,
then numb, so I rubbed it hard. The rubbing didn't help,
though; it just made the pins and needles roll all around
my calf.

Dad bent down to eye level with me on the floor. There
were tears in his eyes too.

"I know it's a shock, honey, but we have to do it. You can
find another ballet school out in the Napa Valley."

"There's no other ballet school!" The entire apartment
building on West 79th Street probably heard me, but my
voice rose up inside my usually gentle soul. "I go to the
Manhattan Dance Company!"

"I know."

"I'm going to be an apprentice in the company . . . I'm
gonna be in the corps of *The Nutcracker* this year . . .
at Lincoln Center!" I started hyperventilating and
couldn't catch my breath. I had worked all my life to be
a ballerina.

Resist! I ordered myself back to sanity. *Don't cry!*

It was no use. I felt like the glossy hardwood floors beneath me were going to cave into the level below, that I would sink all ten floors to the apartment lobby in a crash of wood and steel. My calf muscle went into spasms, and I had to bite my lip to stop from tearing up any more.

"Honey, I know all this," Dad tried to console me. "I do realize the importance of being an apprentice, but what's more important, Kendra—my job or your ballet?"

"My ballet!" The words shot out before I could retract them. I knew I was wrong, but my soul spoke first and reason followed. My head immediately lowered, and I felt terrible for being so selfish.

"Kendra, I won't be able to afford tuition for Manhattan Dance. I won't be able to afford your private school anymore either. Even if we stayed in New York, I couldn't pay for any of that now. Don't you see?"

"No," I whispered through my tears. I didn't see. I wasn't the one who got laid off. Maybe I was selfish. But an adult was telling me whether or not I could be a ballerina. That wasn't fair! Dad had all the control. Why couldn't I have a voice in my own life? Why couldn't I stay in New York to pursue my own dream? My heart broke. "They won't have lights in California," I blurted out in pain.

"What?" Dad didn't understand, but then he looked at the window and muttered a quiet "Oh . . ." He knew. He always knew, I guess. "Talk to you in the morning," he said and disappeared into the bedroom down the dark hallway.

Tears fell faster than I could catch them. As I lay in bed later, they fell from my eyes and ran down the sides of my face, hitting my ears, like heavy dew from a leaf splashing the ground in the morning mist. The stuffing underneath my pillowcase was saturated. I mean, how much water can pour out of your eyes at one time? My chest and lungs hurt. It was hard to breathe. I remembered a story about a saint who cried so much that it made canal lines down his face. I felt like that.

Staring out at the darkness of my bedroom, I saw a sliver of moonlight fall on a picture on the wall. It was a photo of a ballerina tying her pointe shoe. My whole life was ballet, and today had been a good day too. I did twenty fouettés before all this happened, before Dad ruined my life.

With that thought, I rolled over and sobbed into my pillow again. I felt terrible for being so self-centered again. If only I could just feel mad, not guilty or worried about anybody else. But I did. I worried about Dad. I worried about my brother, Petey. I worried about everything all the time, but this move was going to wreck my entire life. Why couldn't Dad see that?

Didn't my life count too?

Did no one care that my soul was about to die if ballet was taken from me?

I turned over and fell into that dead kind of sleep you have when all the sobs have been cried out, when all the muscles have exhausted themselves against a hopeless fight, and when all smiles have been erased from a once joyful heart.

Chapter Two

In the morning, I woke up with dry, puffy eyes, with my eyelashes stuck together from old tears. I reached for my right eye, which I couldn't quite open, and rubbed it clean.

A light breeze blew through my bedroom window and hit the mobile that hung from the ceiling. As I gazed up at the pink figures bouncing above me in the air, ballerinas once again danced before my eyes. The mobile was from the 1970s. It was a relic that belonged to my mother, and even though it was babyish, the mobile was a piece of my mother that I just couldn't give up.

"Give it to your own child when you grow up," she'd said, but the mobile was already falling apart. The leg of one of the figures was ripped from wear, and another ballerina's arm was permanently bent in a backward port de bras. I had watched this childish mobile pirouette and glide ever since I could remember. It was the morning dance that greeted me every day of my life.

The alarm shocked me wide awake and I got up quickly.

A few minutes later in the bathroom, I peeled away the bandages on each of my wrapped toes. The blood-stained bandages on the floor were battle scars. My toes hurt like heck, but I'd broken in new pointe shoes yesterday. Although I'd massaged, bent, banged, and practically bit them to soften them up, walking on demi pointe for hours still made my feet feel like they were going to die. But it was a necessary evil.

A girl in my English class asked me once why I had to beat up my brand-new ballet shoes. She didn't know. Outsiders thought that ballet was all pretty tutus and music, but it took hours and hours of perspiration in classes and rehearsal until I was ready to drop from exhaustion and pain . . . lots and lots of pain.

But the rewards were exquisite! To attain that moment of executing the perfect step in perfect timing with the music and the lights in a performance . . . To reach that total immersion of your being in the dance despite the pain in your feet . . . That was when the magic of ballet truly happened.

My feet would hurt later in class, though.

Before showering, I filled the tub with a mixture of scented body wash and some antibacterial ointment. Cringing, I dipped one foot in, and then the other. The apple pomegranate scent of the body wash made me ignore the sting of the ointment that shot through my red-patched feet. I had to do it to prevent infection. I bore the pain internally, sitting on the side of the tub, looking down at my reddened feet amid the bubbles.

I poured too much bodywash into the tub, but at least my feet would smell good. I tried to laugh, but the joke didn't make me feel better. As I wiggled my toes in the soapy water, I knew that my perfectionism drove me too far.

The whole point of all this pain was to get into Manhattan Dance, but how would I ever get into the company now if we had to move to California?

The smell of breakfast cooking in the kitchen made me want to comfort myself with the eggs and ham that sizzled on the stove. I could smell the slightly burnt toast, just the way Dad and I liked it. But I knew I couldn't eat this morning. The thought of moving to California left my stomach queasy and churning. And Dad had said we were leaving on Friday! That left only one more ballet class. How could I tell Miss Irina?

And why was this all so sudden? There wasn't time to think. Anxiety made me dizzy for a moment, so I tried to block it all out of my mind with the corrections I had to make later at ballet. And I forgot my speech for public speaking was due today at school too.

Stretch the jump, maintain lift, and land like a feather. I made a mental note for my ballet class later, and all the time the ham and burnt toast called out to me, but I had to resist. I was a Spartan warrior.

Endure!

Resist!

Achieve!

"Kendra!" Dad yelled from the kitchen. "Breakfast!"

I got out of the tub, threw my school uniform on, and

was almost out of the apartment before hunger got the best of me and made me steal a piece of toast. Dad turned just in time to see me in the kitchen.

"Kendra! I didn't mean to be so harsh last night." Dad followed me to the door of the apartment. "Kendra?"

I didn't answer him. I was too upset.

"Well, at least eat something!" He looked concerned. "You're sixteen—"

"—and a half," I corrected him, biting on the toast as I headed toward the door.

"You're wasting away to nothing with that ballet. Look at you!"

"I know. I'm a 'stick.'" Dad waved me out the door, and I blew a kiss to Petey in the hallway.

Heading for the elevator, I jumped inside the car with my backpack and pushed the button over and over to close the doors because a woman with a big Newfoundland was running down the apartment hallway.

"Hold the elevator," she cried, but she reached the elevator just as the doors closed.

"Sorry," I called out as the elevator started its downward movement, and I could hear the dog barking from above in the elevator shaft.

The huge dog always scared me. Besides, I just had to be by myself. As soon as the doors closed, I started my daily ritual of self-assessment. The mirrored walls of the elevator reflected a golden but distorted version of me because the golden glass bulged a little. Convex. It was the convex effect of the mirror that made me look fat. I hoped. Did I really look this fat today, or was it these convex, yellow walls?

Exiting the elevator car, I also saw myself in the mirrored lobby. My navy and gray school uniform reflected back, along with the navy school backpack and my black dance bag.

Mirrors were my life.

They followed me throughout the day. The school restrooms, eye makeup mirrors . . . My body reflected in the ballet mirrors after school and later again in my bedroom, where I inspected myself all over again. Did I look good enough? Thin enough? Sometimes I hated the imperfection. A breakout, smudged mascara, a lack of form, an unpointed toe. Was the person in the mirror who searched for utter perfection the real me?

I shrugged and passed Mike, the doorman, as I exited my apartment building. He waved, and I took off down 79th Street.

Madison School for Girls was a short bus ride away. I loved it because professional kids like me had flexible schedules for ballet, acting, or sports as long as we maintained a B grade. But I forgot. I was leaving Madison School for Girls to go to California. Suddenly, it didn't seem so exciting to be able to get out early from school for performances or special master ballet classes that I wouldn't get to take anymore.

The bus took a long time during rush hour in the morning, but I didn't care. I loved New York. How could I ever leave it? The thought of moving made me queasy as I waited for the lumbering M7. The bus roared in and its wheel went onto the curb. All of us at the stop moved back quickly to avoid being hit in its monster path.

"Coulda killed us!" a man shouted, and I nodded.

"Bad driver!" an old woman yelled as the doors opened with a loud squeak.

"Stay out of the way, lady!"

"I'll sue the bus company!" the old woman screamed. I stepped onto the bus, but the driver yelled back.

"The public has to toe the line."

"You run over my foot and I'll sue!" the old lady screamed, and the driver closed the doors in her face. She banged on the doors, but he refused to open them again.

I saw the old woman shake her fist as we pulled away from the curb, and it made me smile. She looked so comical with her fist in the air and that fierce expression on her face contrasting with her frail little body. I then turned my head, and looked out at the stores as we bumped along.

I held onto the hand strap and struggled to find my way to an empty seat. I already felt sick, and I wavered as the bus drove off.

I turned my head and looked out at the stores as we bumped along.

I always had fun people-watching and looking at the stores along Amsterdam Avenue from the window of the bus. Businessmen and actors, designers with portfolios, elderly people, and tourists with kids would get on the bus at the stops. Those who didn't get on walked on the sidewalk with a tunnel-vision purpose. Who were they and where were they all going, walking so fast?

I always wondered, but I knew exactly where I was going—to dance on stage at Manhattan Dance Company. That was the plan before Dad got laid off, before he destroyed my life. I decided to pretend that it was just another normal day, one in which I wouldn't have to tell

Miss Irina that I was leaving Manhattan Dance Company. No, it was just another normal day. I forced myself to look out the window again.

My attention went back to the inside of the bus as two old men on the seats across from me argued about whether you called a yam a sweet potato or whether a yam and a sweet potato were the same thing.

"They have two names!" insisted the one grandpa wearing a blue baseball hat. His face was turning red.

"A yam is not a sweet potato, you idiot!" protested the other grandpa wearing brown trousers and a checked shirt. He stamped his foot, which made the bus floor shake. "I worked at the village farmer's market for thirty-two years, and I know!"

"You know nothing!" The man waved the other one off. The whole thing was stupid, but the old guys asked the opinion of everybody around them, and people took sides. I just laughed because it was a normal bus ride on a normal day in New York City.

At the next stop, the swipe machine for the metro pass on the bus stopped working, so the driver had to call in for repairs. He didn't know when the bus would start again, so I hopped off several blocks ahead of the school to buy hot chocolate from a deli.

The foam of the hot chocolate hit my lips, and right away I felt guilty for giving in to the craving when I resisted the breakfast Dad made. I told the deli man "no whipped cream," but their mistake made me want it even more. I couldn't help myself as the warm liquid inside the cup mixed with the sweet cream and the chocolate taste. My body craved the hot drink, which would help keep my muscles warm and bolster my ballet jumps later in the day. I felt guilty again, though, so I opened the lid, scooped the whipped cream into a street trash basket, and drank only the hot chocolate in the cup. It was my one food luxury for the entire day.

ༀ༚

Inside school, I ran right into Taylor and tried not to spill the rest of my hot chocolate onto both of us.

"You're late!" Taylor tapped her foot like a teacher. She wore the same gray skirt and navy blazer I wore with the Madison School for Girls emblem on the front.

"The bell hasn't rung yet," I said.

"Word has it that you're up for student council," Taylor said.

"I don't have time for student council. I dance." I threw away my empty hot chocolate cup and it went flying into the wastebasket nearby.

"I know. I told them that, but they want to put your name on the ballot anyway."

"Why?"

"It's a joke. They just don't want the president to run again."

"So they pick me? I'd never be able to stand up and speak in front of a bunch of people. " I felt shocked, fearful. I lost my breath for a moment.

"I don't understand how you can dance on stage in front of hundreds of people, but you are too shy in real life."

I shoved my books into my locker and took one back out again. "When I dance, I can be somebody else." I slammed the locker closed. "I can shine, like I told you before." Leaning against the locker, I watched the crowd of girls in their hiked-up gray shirts and navy blazers. "Besides, that's why I like you, Taylor. You're a classical music student, and you're shy just like me."

Two girls in the hallway waved, and I put my head down as a few more walked by. I didn't want to make any eye contact or they might talk me into the student council election, even if it was a joke.

"They've got a petition with your name on the ballot already . . . in the cafeteria."

"Oh no!" I rolled my eyes so far back they got stuck. I blinked quickly.

"I'll come see you practice after class tomorrow," Taylor said, and bolted for the next class. I just put my head down.

How could I tell Taylor that there would be no class tomorrow? My chance in the company . . . The audition that would never happen . . . My dreams . . . Tomorrow would be the night before we left for California.

Tomorrow would be too late.

Chapter Three

After school I turned the corner of West 68th Street and Amsterdam Avenue and walked wearing my school uniform toward Manhattan Dance Company. The street was full of people, as usual. Moms rolled baby prams down the block and across the street and yellow taxis drove on top of one another, but somehow they never crashed. Manhattan Dance was only five blocks away from my private school, so it was a pretty short walk. It was still hot in early September, and the heavy navy blazer of my uniform made me sweat.

A tear rolled down my cheek, and I wiped it away and walked faster. The red light came on at 67th Street, but I crossed anyway, and a whole crowd of people did the same. I almost bumped into a man walking five barking dogs that took up most of the sidewalk, so I moved over to walk on the gray metal grate near the curb. Looking down at the grate under my feet, I heard the roar of the subway train that came up through the sidewalk like a monster, and, not watching, I bumped into a large trash can.

"That was graceful," I chastised myself.

At 66th Street I passed a nice café and wished I could sit down at one of the tables with the large umbrellas and sip a cold iced tea with a lemon on top. The happy people at the café had no troubles. I wanted to be them. They just sat there, watching people like me pass by as they laughed and talked with friends. I bet they didn't have to move to California.

Tears began to stream down the sides of my face, despite my trying to hold them back. Darn. I knew I'd have red, puffy eyes before I even got into class.

Then I saw Lincoln Center stand before me like a familiar friend. I stopped and pondered it with reverence for a long time. It might be the last time I'd ever see it.

It had to be captured. Taking my cell phone out, I snapped a photo of the plaza. I also decided to take a picture of Manhattan Dance from across the street at Lincoln Center. As I jaywalked at the light with another horde of people, I gazed at the street and at the shops that would never ever be part of my daily routine again.

Walking up the steps to the large plaza in front of Lincoln Center, I saw the large David Koch Theater, the Met, the Philharmonic, the Library of the Performing Arts, and Julliard. I then looked back across the street to gaze at Manhattan Dance's building.

"I feel like a tourist," I whispered but focused my camera on the Manhattan Dance sign and clicked. After all, this was the last picture I might ever take of Manhattan Dance too. I had tons of pictures of the ballet school, pictures from the time I was six until just last week, when Liz and I took goofy photos of us there, fighting over a piece of pepperoni pizza. I looked at the ballet school photo on the cell phone, but decided I needed a wider shot.

Stepping back, I refocused the camera.

"Ohhh!"

The next thing I knew, I hit the ground hard. I fell on my right side. It really hurt, and I knew I'd have a huge bruise on my right thigh later.

Looking around, still in my horizontal position, I realized that I slipped on pieces of ice from someone's spilled soda. My cell phone was several feet away from me and the glass screen was cracked. "Huh . . ." I gasped and looked up at the tall Lincoln Center buildings looming above. They looked down at me now, as if mocking me there on the ground. The fall shook my being to its core.

"Are you all right?" A woman stopped to help me, but I nodded I was okay and she left.

"How embarrassing!" I whispered. I was a ballerina, and I fell down in front of Lincoln Center like a royal klutz. Did anyone see me fall? I scrambled to my feet, grabbed my phone, shook shattered bits of glass out of it, and looked over in horror at Manhattan Dance. I could see dancers at the barre through its windows, but felt assured that nobody saw me.

Taking a deep breath, I entered Manhattan Dance. I tried to make myself believe again that it was just an ordinary day. But then I saw myself in the large gilded entryway mirror of the ballet school, possibly for the last time, wearing my Madison School for Girls uniform. A tear threatened to fall again, so I rushed off with my backpack to the dressing room.

Looking inside, I saw dancers getting ready for a class. None of my friends were here yet, since I left school early. It was too early for the company dancers also, which made me sigh with relief and with sadness. I changed my mind about class and went to break the news to Miss Irina instead.

I could see Miss Irina talking with another dance teacher when I knocked at her little office door. She smiled when she saw me.

"Come in, darlink." The office was crowded with files, papers, and pictures of dancers current and past. A pair of bronze pointe shoes sat on her desk, along with a picture of Miss Irina performing with the Kirov.

"Talk to you later," Miss Irina said to the other teacher. "Sit down, Kendra. What can I do for you today?" I paused, unable to speak. The tears falling from my eyes began my story, and Miss Irina got up from her desk to comfort me. "What is it, *Petrushka?*"

I could hardly get the words out, and I didn't remember exactly everything I said. In fact, I don't remember any of it, except for Miss Irina crooning, "Is terrible!" over and over.

I shook my head. "And we leave tomorrow," I sobbed.

"Is an injustice!" Miss Irina spoke sternly, as though she was reliving the Bolshevik Revolution, which she was much too young to have experienced. But I knew what she meant. She always said I had potential to be a soloist in the company. Now my chance would be zero.

"What am I going to do?" I blew my nose into a tissue.

"There is nothink you can do. Your fadder take you away." Miss Irina hesitated, then continued. "My prize pupil . . . You come back, yes?"

I shook my head. Both of us knew that me returning may never be in the cards.

"Miss Irina, what am I going to do?" Miss Irina hugged me hard, and we both let out a heart-wrenching sigh together.

Chapter Four

O n the plane to California, I stared out the window. I saw the mountains in the west below and thought of the "purple mountains' majesty" from the song. It was true. The mountains in the west really were purple. It was no comfort, though. As we flew over the scenery, I felt my life slipping away before my eyes.

I knew that adults were the bosses until you were legally of age, but there were times when a person had to make a decision that would affect his or her entire life. Ballet careers started at the age of sixteen. I needed to dance in New York *now*, but why couldn't Dad see that?

Petey, wearing his usual red and green clothes, decided to have a tantrum. Dad was in the seat across from me and tried to help Petey. Annoyed, I grabbed my brother and put him on my lap. It immediately quieted him down, and he sucked his thumb and fell asleep from boredom.

"What am I going to do?" I spoke aloud but Dad didn't hear me. The white noise of the plane drowned out the small sound from my distraught soul.

Every morning at seven thirty, I sat in homeroom at Madison School for Girls. At two o'clock, I walked the five blocks to take class at Manhattan Dance. Every day. Every single day of my life. What would I do now?

Would Taylor and Liz forget all about me? Would I find new best friends? My heart raced with anxiety and I felt panicked. Would I have any friends at all in the new school? There'd be over a thousand students there. A thousand! There were only ninety-nine girls at Madison. My stomach tightened.

The most important thing was that I had to find a ballet class in California as soon as possible. I had to formulate a plan.

San Francisco had a good ballet company, I remembered. So did Los Angeles. I knew some girls who trained in LA and then came to Manhattan Dance. How far was San Francisco or Los Angeles from where we'd be? I'd find out. There might be good teachers in our new city too. I decided to research it all as soon as I got settled. I'd search the Internet and by cell and I'd find a ballet teacher like Miss Irina.

I had to, or my life would be over. The white noise of the plane drowned out even my thoughts and I fell asleep from exhaustion. Dad's hand shook my shoulder.

"What time is it?" I mumbled. Petey woke up too. He was still on my lap.

"We're in San Francisco," Dad said. "Hold Petey's hand tight. We'll get the bags first and then get the car." Petey opened his eyes slowly, and I looked out the window to see airport fuel trucks and baggage workers driving around. I couldn't see anything that looked like pictures of San Francisco. All I saw was airport and the rain drizzling from the sky.

As we grabbed our bags at the baggage claim, Dad led us out the doors and we got on an airport shuttle that was full of people.

"Executive Rent-A-Car," Dad said to the driver of the shuttle.

"How much farther do we have to go?" I asked.

"Fifty-five miles, I think," Dad said. "It'll be another hour or so before we get there, if there's no traffic."

"Where are you going?" the driver asked.

"Napa Valley. What's the best way to get there?" The driver made a sharp right turn and we held on until he straightened the shuttle out again.

"Well, the most direct way is to take the Interstate 80–Bay Bridge route to wine country."

"Okay," Dad said, writing it down.

"But if it's busier, like it is now, you might want to take the Interstate 280 Highway across the Golden Gate Bridge, route one north . . ."

"Oh," Dad said and crossed out the previous instruction. "Thanks," he said, and we got off a few minutes later at the car rental place.

Not long after that we drove across the famous Golden Gate Bridge. The steel girders and suspension ropes hung above me and I leaned my head out the window until Dad stopped me.

"Stay inside, please," he said, so I looked over at the big office buildings and looked for the famous hilly streets. I couldn't see anything up close, but the view was great.

I looked back down at the water. There were seals on the rocks below, and I couldn't believe my eyes. These seals weren't in a zoo—they were wild. The trip definitely was worth it, just to see the baby seals.

An hour later, the California sun beat down its strong September heat as Dad drove the rented, black Lexus along the highway. Even though he insisted he knew the way, of course we got lost. We stopped to eat at a restaurant for dinner because we had no food in our new house, Dad said, but the real reason was that he needed to get directions.

"Come on," Dad said as we finished our hamburgers. "We're going home."

Home? My heart dropped inside my chest. My home was New York. Now I was going to a house. It would never be my real home—not in a million years.

We left the highway and headed onto a country road. A pickup truck full of farm equipment passed us, and I saw a sign that read, "Welcome to Apple Glen." My heart sank. We weren't just going to live in a house; we were going to live in Hicksville too. We passed field after field of farms.

The sun was setting, and it cast an orange-reddish glow over the whole sky and over the fields. It was kind of like that painting I saw once at the Guggenheim museum on a school field trip, where farmers worked in the fields and the sky was a blaze of sunset colors, and the brush strokes streaked all over the painting.

"Grapes," Dad said, pointing. I looked closer to see if I could find the grapes, but they were too far away. "We're in wine country. Napa Valley."

I didn't say anything, just took in the green fields with rows between the lines of grapevines. We went down an even narrower road.

There were farmhouses with more fields and even more grapes. One field extended right to the edge of the road, and I got a close-up of the grapevines. The purple grapes hung in large bunches beneath green covers of leaves, which streaked orange-red from the setting summer sun. I had never seen a real live crop before.

"And look at the houses." Dad pointed again. The houses were really nice, not ramshackle farmhouses at all, but large estates.

"Farmers must make a lot of money around here."

"Really expensive," Dad continued. "Big money here, big industry here. We're lucky my company found us a place."

I looked out the window again at the passing estates and vineyards. It was like being in another country, like France, surrounded by all these grapes. Petey grunted in the backseat, and I turned around to grab his foot. He pointed at a bird that sat on top of a grapevine post.

"Bird, Petey." I nudged him. "Say *bird.*" Petey grunted again and looked away.

I looked away too, and a great sadness overwhelmed me. I stared in silence out the window at the passing scenery. There was one farm after another. They all looked the same, with the same annoying orange-red sunset in the background. Like those paintings in the museum, I would be one of those brush-streaked characters in them. I'd be forced to live within the boundaries of the frame that somebody else made, and I would never get out.

∽✺∼

Ten minutes later, I stood in front of our new house. It looked like a house from one of those TV sitcom shows where a perfect family lived—the kind where the teens all knew exactly what to say and had families with no problems that couldn't be resolved in a half hour of viewing. It was . . .

"Big," I said.

"Quite a change from New York, eh?" Dad smiled but then knew he'd said the wrong thing.

"Can we afford it?" Now I said the wrong thing. I felt terrible.

"Super Symmetry Computers invested in real estate and they have a few of these houses for executive rentals. If we like it, I can rent–buy it from a real estate agent later on." Dad pinched my cheek as if I were a five-year-old. "Like I told you, we're lucky. I'd never be able to afford this now on my reduced salary." He sighed. "Well, maybe after a promotion."

I knew I should have been grateful for such a beautiful house. There were no trees, and the lawns had no grass yet because no one ever lived there before. There would be no more elevators, apartment laundry machines, big Newfoundland dogs, and Mike, the doorman. I chewed on my cheek and tried to be positive.

"It's beautiful," I replied, staring into the house through the open door. "And the stairs inside aren't too steep for Petey. He'll be able to climb them."

"I'm glad you like it." Dad grabbed my arm. "Look at the street sign." I looked up to see the burgundy-colored street sign at the corner. Its white lettering read *Pinot* and *Bordeaux.*

"Our address is . . ."

"202 Bordeaux Lane. The development's theme is . . ."

"Types of wines?"

"We had the option of a house on Champagne or Cabernet—"

"Cabaret? Like the musical?"

"No, Cabernaayyy. It's a wine." Dad then hit his chest, kind of like a gorilla, and looked up at the California sun. "Nice weather," he said and beat his chest again. Dad could be so weird at times. I still loved him, though, and I could tell he was excited about the move. How could I tell him that he was tearing my heart apart by forcing me away from New York?

"Don't you miss it?" I looked up at him. "The city?"

"We have to make changes sometimes in life," he said. "We'll visit someday, after we get settled. Next year, maybe."

"That's a long time," I said.

"Yeah, well . . . Wait'll you see your room, honey." Dad changed the subject. "It's huge, and it's all ready for you. I paid the workmen extra to set some of your stuff up in advance."

"The workmen touched my stuff?" I was horrified. I ran upstairs and was amazed when I looked around my bedroom.

He was right. My room was huge. In fact, though I hated to admit it, my room was perfect. Even though it was filled with stacks of shipping boxes, I could see that it had a large mirrored closet and enough room for me to do ballet. My furniture fit better in here than it did in the smaller New York City apartment. I actually had some space. As I stared at the pale pink walls with white edging, I noticed it was almost as if Dad tried to make it look like the inside of Manhattan Dance with its peach walls and white moldings. Suddenly, the workmen touching my stuff didn't seem like such a big deal anymore when I saw how much Dad had really tried.

"Thanks, Dad," I mumbled.

"Look around for a few minutes. Settle in. Then come see Petey's room." Dad picked Petey up and left for the other bedroom.

As I looked at the mirrored wall, I realized that there would be plenty of room for me to do barre work and even a tour jeté or two in the middle of the room. I tried it for good measure and fit in two neat tour jetés, but then I almost fell over a box, because my bruised thigh was still a battle scar, like my broken heart and my bleeding toes.

Hesitant to try out any more ballet moves just yet, I sat down on the bed with my puffy, beige comforter. Above the bed I saw my old, pink mobile reinstalled in a new place. The two odd ballerinas with a missing leg and a bent arm still twirled, despite the injuries caused by years of wear. It was as though they weren't even aware that we had moved. They danced their odd dance as they always did, and I lay down on the bed and stared up at them. Somehow it comforted me, seeing them again.

As I looked around the room, I remembered my plan and grabbed my computer. I had to look up dance studios and ballet stores for leotard replacements. I had to get my resources set.

"Kendra?" Dad called me from the other room. "Come see Petey's room."

I sighed. *Petey.* Here I was, wallowing in my own misery, and I hadn't even spared a thought for how this change would be affecting my little brother. I felt a twinge of guilt. "Coming," I yelled and closed the laptop again.

Getting up again, I walked down the hall to Petey's room. Petey grunted several times, so I knew he was experiencing anxiety. He always did that in new places. I popped my head in and saw Petey's room, which was set up with furniture, old and new.

"When did you do all this?" I asked. I automatically took Petey by the hand, and he quieted down.

"I wanted to surprise you. I had the workmen set it up for Petey too. They painted both your rooms and put new furniture in."

"But how did they have enough time?" My voice trailed off as I realized the sad truth. "You've known about the move for a long time, haven't you?" My head lowered, and I felt betrayed.

"I just couldn't bring myself to tell you, Kendra. Your ballet and all . . ." I put my hand on Dad's shoulder, because he looked a little unsteady now.

"The rooms do look nice," I said, changing the subject.

"My room still needs work, and it smells too strongly of fresh paint. We'll open all the windows to air it out." I sat down on Petey's bed as Dad opened his window. I turned on his new bed lamp, which was shaped like a train, but Petey screamed and held his ears, so I clicked it off again.

"He'll have to get used to the new lamp."

"He can sleep in bed with you for a while, 'til he gets used to it all."

"If he does get used to it . . ." My thoughts trailed off.

"He will." Dad looked a little unsure, though, as Petey sat rocking on the floor, heavy with fear. "I'll get Petey an autism aide who also does light housekeeping. It's a big place."

"Too soon. He has to get adjusted to the new environment first. It would be too much to get him an aide all at once."

"You're probably right, but we'll have to do something. You have to go to school, young lady, and I have to go to work." I knew this was true, but Petey would react badly. I knew it, and just when I was making so much progress with his clapping games back in New York. This could set Petey back years.

"School starts tomorrow. The bus comes at 7:15. If you miss it, there's a second one at 7:40, the school told me, but you'll be late on that one. The school is five miles away."

"Five miles!"

"It's all on one long country road. Chapel Street, I think. Gotta get used to the new street names around here." Dad scratched his head and left the room.

I didn't get up from Petey's bed right away. Instead, I sat thinking about all the people I had to meet at the new school in the morning. My heart raced as I imagined the monster of a school with its thousand students waiting to eat me alive.

⚘

The school bus arrived promptly at 7:15 the next morning and I got on. It was half full already, and loud. I grabbed a seat and put my backpack on the adjoining one to be alone.

"Partyyyy!" someone screamed. "My house . . . next Friday!"

The bus started, then stopped to let on a late passenger. It started with a jerk again, and we rode out of the development onto Chapel Street, where it began the long, bumpy, five-mile ride.

We stopped here and there to pick up farm kids. Unfortunately, the bus filled up quickly, and a few minutes later, the empty seat next to me was taken by another girl who moved my backpack onto the dirty floor.

"I don't know you." The girl had long, blonde, slightly frizzy hair and a few freckles on her cheeks. "I'm back here!" she shouted to some guy on the bus. He waved, acknowledging her.

"I'm new," I said and looked back out the window. I didn't feel like talking to people I didn't know.

"Where you from?"

"Madison," I said.

"Wisconsin?"

"No, New York," I said and looked out the window again.

I saw some vegetable stands on the side of the road as we passed, and I saw fresh produce that looked incredibly big. The eggplants and cucumbers and tomatoes were larger than any I'd ever seen back in New York at Delmonico's supermarket, and Delmonico's had the best. I couldn't believe my eyes as I saw the fruit that sat in little cardboard boxes on stands as we flew by on the rickety bus.

"Oh my gosh! My nails are starting to curve in." The girl beside me freaked out. "That's supposed to be a symptom of, like, anemia or something." The girl showed me her nails.

"They look all right to me," I said, glancing at them.

"I saw it on a medical show last night—scoopy nails." The girl seemed too young to be a hypochondriac, but she sure was acting like one. I turned to look out the window, but she pestered me again.

"You don't think it's anything serious, do you?"

"I'm sure you'll be fine," I said. I wanted to smile. She was a pretty girl but a little high-strung. "My name's Kendra Sutton," I said, hoping to get her mind off her scoopy nails.

"I'm Becca." Becca looked with worry at her nails once more, and then, thankfully, took out a paperback novel and began to read. Since I was free to stare out the window again, I looked at the sights.

Out the window, I saw another stand selling weird tubular plants with holes and more pumpkins. There were vineyards that went on forever too—miles and miles.

I remembered my daily bus ride in New York, where I saw all kinds of people getting on and off the bus, where I saw interesting stores every day, and nothing ever, ever got boring. I remembered people reading the *New York Times* or the *Wall Street Journal*, folding them in that funny, long fold so they didn't hit the people beside them with the paper. I remembered the colorful people and the funny things they did, like the old men arguing about yams and sweet potatoes.

I also remembered that I was now in California, a state that wasn't my home. Back in New York, it would be three hours later, and I would be at Madison School for Girls. And then in a few hours, I'd be in class with Miss Irina . . .

"Jerk!" A backpack went flying by me, barely missing my head, and a younger kid ran back to retrieve it. "Sit in the back of the bus!"

"Make me, twinkle toes!"

"Troy! Don't!" Becca shouted to an older, cute guy with sandy blond hair who followed the younger one. The cute guy chased the kid down the aisle, but the younger one slipped as the bus rattled and shook. The bus driver yelled at everyone to "sit down!" As the two boys quieted and took seats far apart, I looked in disgust at the older bully, who turned around, looked in my direction, and smiled. I turned my face away again and looked out the window once more.

This was shaping up to be the worst day ever. I took a deep breath and told myself I was on a vacation for a week, and that I'd return next Sunday to New York, ready to take ballet class. Yes, I was just on vacation . . . wasn't I?

It was a lie, but the lie saved me from dying on the bus that day.

Chapter Five

When the bus pulled into the school parking lot, I got off and looked around at Seneca High School. Several girls pointed at me for some reason and laughed. I realized that they were laughing at my outfit. I wore a black blazer, a black tee, and nice jeans since there was no dress code. Why were they pointing at me?

Looking up at the large building that loomed in front of me, I felt intimidated by the steel and glass structure that had several smaller structures attached to it. Even though I saw skyscrapers in New York, somehow this short but sprawling building made me scared. It was X, the unknown factor.

I glanced over at the football field, and then to my left, where I saw the track. Loud music sounded in my ears and I realized that it was the school band, practicing on the field. The two girls who laughed at my outfit were cheer-leaders in purple and yellow uniforms, and they paraded with the band. Later, everyone went into the school, some quickly and others more reluctantly.

Walking down the hallway, I read my schedule and looked for room 116—homeroom. I saw room 112, 114, and 118, but there was no room 116. I circled back, thinking I missed it, but again I couldn't find it. I tried to ask a passing student, but the girl ignored me, heading for a guy, obviously her boyfriend, hanging at her locker.

Locker! I forgot I had one. I looked at the locker number. It was number 515. I rushed down the hallway and found mine at the other end, threw some of my books in there, then ran back with my backpack to find room 116 again. The bell rang and students disappeared into the classrooms, leaving me and another student all alone in the hall. The boy looked at me and then left the building, truant.

"Do you have a hall pass?" I turned around, startled to see a teacher.

"I'm looking for my homeroom. It's my first day." The man looked at my registration slip and said, "Down the hall." He pointed and then left. Great! I knew that already, but there was no room 116. Maybe it only materialized on certain days of the week. I tried to keep my sense of humor as I walked up the hall again with my books and opened the door to room 114.

"Excuse me. Is this 116?"

"No!" the students shouted. I closed the door without apology. I leaned against the hallway wall, and tears welled up in my eyes from embarrassment.

"Do you have a hall pass?" It was another teacher.

"No," I cried out. "I'm late for school, went into the wrong classroom. I'm not supposed to be in California at all and . . . and . . . I have to find room 116!"

"Is that all? Room 112 is now room 116. Students still get confused about that change."

"Of course!" I pretended I forgot. "Thanks." I wiped my eyes and slipped into room 116, the former 112.

"You're late!" a male teacher said. "Don't make it a habit."

I looked around the room. There were twenty-five or twenty-six students; I counted them quickly. They all looked at me as if I were a circus clown.

"You're the new girl . . . uh . . ." The teacher looked at his roster. "Ms. Sutton?"

I nodded, and all of the students looked at me.

"What're you wearing?" a girl said.

"I like it," said a boy.

"Me too," said another girl.

"She dresses like my mom!" The first girl got hysterical, and everybody laughed.

"What do *you* know?" another girl shouted back at the first. "Miss Queen of Fashion?"

"All right. That's enough!" The teacher calmed the room down.

I wanted to die. All the fuss about my clothes put a spotlight on me, the kind I didn't want. It was the cheerleader again. Dressed like someone's mother? Not knowing what the uniform was here, I'd worn an outfit like my old school uniform from Madison School for Girls. It was the kiss of death here at Seneca for some reason. The bus wouldn't be back again until three, so I'd have to suffer through it for the rest of the day. I slunk into a spare seat, trying not to cry for the millionth time this week.

One of the guys in class noticed me and smiled. He wore a navy sweater vest and a white shirt. He readjusted his designer eyeglasses, ran his fingers through his ginger-brown hair, and then looked back down at his notebook. I took a seat just in time for the bell to ring for the end of homeroom. Well, at least there was one nice thing in this awful school—the ginger-brown-haired guy.

At lunch the cafeteria was crowded. I ditched the blazer in my locker along the way, hoping that my outfit would look more normal, but my arms were so thin that they stuck out of the black tee like twigs, which made me feel even shyer. What made it even worse was that my body shook with the clatter and the bigness of the school. And I still had to test survival skills in the cafeteria.

The food line was packed with the high school cliques—jocks, nerds, geeks, rockers, pops, wallflowers, weirdos, and the brains . . . I wasn't sure how the kids would treat me at this school, so I passed by warily and I tiptoed past the goths to avoid any eye contact.

The lunch lady dished the food out like gruel from Oliver Twist's workhouse. It didn't look anything like the food at my other school. Thin-sauced chili, drippy mac and cheese. Ugh. And it didn't even look like the Californian food I'd heard about. There were no healthy-looking salads in the food line that I could see.

I glanced at mystery meat burgers and overdone hot dogs. The smell was atrocious. The whole school reeked of the gym, and the odor permeated the cafeteria too. It smelled like old socks and sweaty burgers wrapped up in one. I wanted to hurl. Suddenly I wished that I brought my own lunch and then decided to choose a little salad I spied at the end. What could they do to a salad?

I shouldn't have asked. The lettuce on the chef salad was the white, hard part of the lettuce and the tomatoes were unripe, not at all like the great tomatoes I saw during the bus ride. The ham, cheese, and turkey were processed like the pressed meat people bought in a can. I was glad I brought an energy bar with me. Tossing the salad into the trash, I felt better eating the protein bar. It was comfort food, because it reminded me of Manhattan Dance and Miss Irina.

"New?"

The question scared me. Who was asking? Would I give the right answer or would I blow it like my clown outfit? I turned to see the cheerleader from homeroom standing beside me. She sat down, flipped her hair, and asked again. "New?"

"What do you care?" I responded. "Apparently I dress like your mom." I lowered my eyes. It hurt a lot, especially when I wanted to look good for my first day. My heart sank as I thought of mom. She would have had good advice for me now. She'd know what to say to this girl. But she was gone.

The cheerleader's smile faded a little. "Sorry about that. You just looked so . . . prep school."

I went back to my energy bar. I shook my head, unsure of the California lingo, but then figured I'd have to talk sometime. "I did go to a prep school. Just moved from New York."

"Oh." The cheerleader nodded. "What'd you do there?"

I was afraid to answer, but it actually felt good to speak to someone. "I did ballet and went to private school."

Several friends of the cheerleader sat down also. They also appeared to be cheerleaders since they wore the purple-and-yellow school logo, a lion.

"She's a ballet dancer from New York," the first cheerleader said. She turned back to me. "I'm Bailey Adams."

"Kendra Sutton." I felt a little uncomfortable as the girls eyed me like an oddity.

"So, what did you do for fun there?"

"Ballet. My dad and I'd go to the theater. I went to the opera last week . . ."

"Oh." Bailey's conversation stopped dead, and I could see her mind going into overdrive. "Well, we'll see you later," she said and motioned for her friends to follow her. As they walked away, they began whispering and laughing hysterically to one another. They sat down at a table nearby, and I could hear snippets of their conversation.

"Opera!" Bailey Adams whispered it, but screamed in laughter. "Let's call her 'Opera Girl,'" she said. The words were meant for me to hear. Bailey looked over at me, then glanced away again. "Opera Girl," the others echoed and laughed. "Come on, let's go," Bailey said to her drones. "She's too high class for us." Bailey lowered her voice once again, whispering, but I could hear every word. "Besides, we don't need more competition."

I could hear them laughing all the way through the cafeteria and out the door. I heard them scream with laughter again outside the glass doors in the quad. My face flushed and felt hot. It wasn't fair. Nasty Bailey Adams didn't even let me finish my sentence.

"It's okay if you like opera," I heard a small, quiet voice say behind me. Turning, I saw one of the goth girls standing before me. At first it startled me, but her soft-spoken voice calmed me again. "Everyone has a right to like what they want." The girl sat down. I didn't know what to say, so I just managed a small "Oh."

"Don't mind Bailey Adams. She's a . . ." Almost hearing the "B" word come out of that soft-spoken, serene voice made me burst out laughing. "My name's Sylvan." The girl smiled. Even though she was different from me, she didn't appear to be mean like those cheerleaders. Plus, I was different from everybody else in this school apparently, so who was I to judge? I decided to talk to her.

"I'm Kendra . . . Sutton." I looked up at her for a brief moment. "Actually, I hate opera. I was just going to tell Miss Bailey Adams that I went to see my friend, Liz, dance in the ballet of the opera *La Gioconda*. She danced the part of 'Evening' in the 'Dance of the Hours.'"

"Evening? Was there a morning dance too?"

Now I looked back up, because Sylvan seemed genuinely interested.

"And 'Afternoon' and 'Night.' It was kind of fun to see." I smiled when I remembered Liz in the show. "I endured the boring singing part of it all just to see Liz do her part . . . but I hate opera."

"But you love ballet!" Sylvan smiled. She looked kind of sweet when she smiled. She was short, petite, and had a white flower in her dyed-black hair that matched her all-black tee, skirt, and tights. Her white eye makeup matched the flower. The goth table waved over to Sylvan, impatient. "I'll come talk to you again," she said with her soft voice and left.

I got up from the table and went straight to the girls' room. As I left the cafeteria, many eyes were still upon me, and their voices rang in my ears.

"Who's the new girl?"

"What's she all about?"

"She doesn't look like a goth."

I heard the whisperings as I, the new flavor of the month, set the cafeteria all abuzz. I walked to the girls' room, trying to be incognito. Unfortunately, the girls' room was full of girls sneaking smokes and putting on makeup. One of the stalls overflowed and I had to sidestep the stream of water that ran down the middle of the room. I left in disgust and went to my next class early. The classroom was empty, so I sat alone in blissful peace to finish my energy bar.

I missed Miss Irina and Madison School for Girls.

After school, I ran into the house and flew up the stairs, almost knocking Petey over. Petey followed me up the stairs, but I slammed the door shut before he reached it. He banged on the door with his fist.

"Go away!" He stopped banging but still stood there.

"Uh," I could hear him grunting outside the door. Feeling guilty, I opened the door again and let him in. He ran right to the bed and sat down to watch me silently, rocking slowly and rhythmically.

The tears were about to drop again, but I pulled them back, trying hard not to cry in front of Petey. I lost the war, though. The tears poured down my cheeks because of my miserable day, but Petey reached up to touch my face. It startled me. He usually withdrew from touch of any kind and didn't touch others back.

Looking up at him through the teary water, my eyelashes became little prisms of light forming a rainbow over my lids. It seemed poetic somehow, like a tragic ballet, but then Petey grunted and the illusion melted. He knew something was wrong. I dried my tears and turned to my brother.

"Do you want me to read you a story?" He stopped rocking and grunting, then sat silently, waiting.

He looked so small for a six-year-old and so strange in his usual red shirt and green shorts, a constant reminder of his autism. Why he picked red and green, we didn't know, but he wouldn't wear any other color. Just shopping for him at the store was a pain in the butt. We could only buy red this or green that, and sometimes it was hard to find anything red or green in his size.

"He looks like a Christmas tree," Dad always said.

I grabbed a children's book from my closet, one from my stack of childhood picture books that I still couldn't bear to throw out. But then I remembered my computer. I put the book back down on the bed and opened the laptop to a folder marked "Ballet." I clicked and the folder opened to display photos of others and myself in various costumes.

"I'll tell you a fairy tale," I said. Gathering Petey, we sat together on the bed. I showed my brother the photos, one by one. "This is Sleeping Beauty," I said and pointed to my Aurora ballet costume. "And this is me as Clara in *The Nutcracker*." Petey grunted several times in quick succession, which meant he liked the photos. He liked them because I was in them. "This is the Mouse King," I said, pointing to the photo. "He is very bad." Petey grunted once more, listening. "And here I am as Giselle, and here is me as a white swan, and as a snowflake," I said with a smile. I hadn't smiled in over a week.

Petey enjoyed the pictures, I could tell. He moved his arms and legs around, not in coordinated movement, but almost uncontrolled as he looked at the photos, which meant that he was contented. "And here I am as a Sugar Plum Fairy. It's a very sparkly costume."

His eyes were very attentive. He looked up at me and locked eyes, then threw himself against me and closed his eyes. He had this knack of falling asleep without warning, almost like a narcoleptic. I carefully picked him up and laid him in his own bed, then went back to my room.

The e-photo album was still open on my computer, showcasing me as the Sugar Plum Fairy. Looking at it I smiled, but then I started to sob.

"Kendra?" I looked up. It was Dad at my door. "Are you all right?"

"No!" I said. "I want to be back in New York!" My sobs worsened and I couldn't hold them in.

"You will someday." Dad stood in the doorway and sighed. "You've got the audition in the spring."

"I won't be in good enough shape in the spring if I'm not at Manhattan Dance *now*!"

"You'll find a good ballet school here somewhere. I'm sure—"

"I could live with Miss Irina," I interrupted, my eyes wide open. Almost crazed with my tragic situation, I clung to this idea.

"Miss Irina would never let you do that." Dad waved his hand. "Forget it."

"Miss Irina *loves* me!" I shouted back. "I should have asked her before I left."

"Don't get any ideas, Kendra."

"I'll email her right now," I said, wiping my tears away from my cheeks. "If she says okay, can I do it?" I looked at Dad in earnest. "Can I live with Miss Irina?"

"She won't let you, Kendra." Dad sighed heavily again. "Miss Irina only cares about the money. You are good, Kendra, but they can replace you in a minute with another girl. She's probably found another prize pupil already."

"That's not true!" I typed Miss Irina's email into the address bar as I spoke. "Gymnasts and ice skaters live with their coaches away from home. Ballet dancers can too." I typed furiously.

"Miss Irina won't let you," Dad stated again.

"If she says yes will you let me?" Dad put his head in his hands and looked up at me. "Will you let me?" I repeated. Dad then looked up at the ceiling.

"If she for any reason, which I cannot fathom, allows you to live with her . . ." He paused and turned from me away for a moment. I realized then that I hurt Dad bad. I chose Miss Irina over him. It never even occurred to me that he'd feel that way. After all, it was a good solution, wasn't it?

Now I wasn't so sure. Dad almost looked like he was going to cry when he turned back toward me. My heart felt like it sunk to the bottom of the earth. And there was Petey to think about too. How could I forget about Petey? Was I being selfish because I wanted to dance? I was about to call the whole thing off when Dad said, "I guess it's fine with me."

"Okay, " I said, quietly because Petey was asleep. "It would only be for a few months, until the audition."

"But, Kendra . . . don't get your hopes up." I ignored his warning as he walked away. I was on a mission to get back to New York. "Miss Irina loves me," I whispered as I hit the Send button and propelled the email into cyberspace.

What did Dad know about Miss Irina anyway? Miss Irina always said that she was related to the Romanovs, the last royal family of Russia, but Dad said that she probably fibbed about that. He also said that if she was really related, it was probably to a fifth cousin, twenty-seven times removed. He was biased. He didn't know how much I meant to her. Thinking about Miss Irina made me even more homesick.

"At my country, we sing all the day to make the dance. After Kirov, I come to America and another success make!" The memory of her voice made me smile. "Keep fouettés crisp, like chip," she always said.

A tear rolled from my eye. My heart missed her so much. Then I remembered my plan to live with her. I smiled and threw myself back down on my pillow against the headboard and sighed a huge sigh of relief. "*Spasibo*." That's what I would tell her if she let me live with her. "Thank you." I may just have found my ticket out of this maze of grapes. But the thought of Petey, so small and vulnerable, crept into my mind, and no matter how hard I tried, I couldn't shake it.

Bordeaux Street turned into Pinot Avenue, and then Pinot turned into Champagne, then out to the main drag— Chapel Street. As I looked out the car window at our new Napa Valley town the next afternoon, I saw the rugged country roads that eventually turned into paved roads, and the beautiful suburban homes that lined the streets as we drove by. I could see from the road that many of the homes had vineyards behind them. But the no-man's-land continued as we hit yet another cluster of vineyards. I played with the windshield's sun visor, trying to adjust it.

"Don't be so rough," my dad said. He was just as frustrated as me, only for a different reason. He'd gotten lost the other night, and from the way he touched his forehead, I could tell we might be lost again. "It must be this way," he muttered.

There were a lot of grapes, and truthfully, the fields were beautiful. I'd never seen country like this before, but after miles of farmland, it got boring really fast. I felt guilty for calling it a no-man's-land in my head, but as we drove along, the grapes rose up to meet us like that Irish saying, welcoming us to the Napa Valley, only I was way too young to drink the wine that they were so famous for. Maybe Napa Valley was good for adults, but for kids it was a desert of nothing but forbidden fruit.

"Is this all that's here?" I asked as I peered out the window.

"Give it a chance, hon. It's a nice place, I hear."

"Well, when I'm back in New York, you can write about it."

"Have you heard from Miss Irina?" Dad posed the question, and I suddenly went silent. I didn't want to answer it. It had been days since I sent the email. I checked and rechecked the computer twenty times a day for her response. But there was none. As a matter of fact, I hadn't heard from Liz, my best friend, either. The reality of both made me feel sad.

"She's probably out at the Hamptons on vacation." My voice shook, but I covered well. Inside, I worried. Dad's face registered a look of "I told you so," but he tried hard not to let it show.

We turned into Apple Glen proper, and Dad drove into a large shopping center that had a supermarket, several restaurants, a big nursery, a lumber place, a Laundromat, a convenience store, a hair stylist, and other smaller shops. Well, at least there was something to look at here in Apple Glen. From the backseat, Petey unleashed a hard kick, right into my back.

"Ow! Stop it, Petey!"

Petey looked wounded that I yelled at him, and my eyes widened.

"He showed emotion, Dad." Dad turned the ignition off and looked back at Petey, who was stoic and began to rock.

"Nah, it's just gas."

"Dad!" I turned back to Petey again. "I'm sorry, Petey." I caught his foot and squeezed it, and Petey calmed down and stared out the window without any further reaction.

"Well, here it is," he exclaimed proudly."

"What?" I was confused.

"There's a dance school—The American Dance Centre—over there." I looked in the direction he indicated and sure enough, there was a dance school. I blinked.

"Wait . . . what? I don't have my dance bag."

"Right here." Dad picked up my dance bag from the backseat and threw me a brochure. "Here's the schedule. They have an advanced class that starts right about . . . now. We'll wait," he said. He winked at my stunned expression. I couldn't believe how nice Dad was to do this, especially after I almost threw him over for Miss Irina.

"You drove us all the way into town just so I could try a new dance studio?" I felt like I wanted to cry all over again, but for a good reason this time. I shot Dad one last look of gratitude before grabbing my dance bag and exiting the car. I blew a small kiss to Petey and ran into the ballet school.

Inside, a woman sat at a desk, collecting money from students. There was a rack of brochures next to the desk, and a wall of photos of the school recitals and individual dancers. There was a small dance shop to the left that sold dancewear, bookends, tee shirts, pins, and glittery barrettes, all mostly in pink with little ballet shoes all over them. On my right I saw two classes in session, a tap class and a jazz. On my left there was a class of toddlers moving with a great lack of rhythm to music. I heard applause from another room nearby. The dancers exited that class quickly and others piled in. It was a factory school.

I approached the woman at the desk. "Single class," I stated. "Advanced Ballet."

"Advanced Ballet is by invitation only." The woman eyed me. She was old, probably around forty, and she wore a lot of eye makeup. "I teach the class."

"I can do it," I said and plopped the money down on the desk. I disappeared into the ladies room to change before she could protest.

Ten minutes later, I walked into the class and saw a bevy of girls from ages eleven to eighteen. I watched them in the mirror as they talked and moved around in the dancewear they bought from the shop, some wearing glittery bows in ponytails and others in pink or electric-blue leotards with black tights. That would never have been allowed at Manhattan Dance Company. Black leotard, pink tights, hair in a bun . . . I wanted to leave but forced myself to knock it off. This could be my only way to train for the spring audition.

"Ms. Oakman!" All of the girls began to jump up and down, fawning over the woman at the desk, who was obviously the owner of the school, Sheila Oakman. The sycophant girls made me sick as they surrounded Ms. Oakman, who was now dressed in a black leotard and black dance skirt. The woman's credits hung on one wall of the ballet room. She had been a Rockette. There were pictures of her in the kick line at Radio City Music Hall in New York, on tour and dressed as a wooden soldier and as a candy cane.

"At the barre, girls." Sheila Oakman turned on the boom box, and it blared distorted music from Tchaikovsky.

I remembered the pianist who played Tchaikovsky in New York. He was a student from Julliard, a thin, little guy with heavy, black glasses who played for our classes. Live music trained you, Manhattan Dance said, to capture movement more realistically, and it prepared you for orchestra. But here in the Sheila Oakman Boom Box Hall of Fame, the tinny sound guided our steps like the wooden soldiers in the pictures on the wall.

The barre work went too swiftly, and I moved to center

floor. The other girls were not advanced, and I didn't want to show off, so I faltered on a fouetté. One girl I noticed did have good extension and strength, and I smiled at her. She smiled a friendly smile in return.

Ten minutes before class ended, the boom box music stalled, so as I waited, I looked in the mirror. I remembered the golden mirror from the elevator in New York, but now I had no barometer to assess my weight. Was I still thin enough? I stretched my pointe hard as I wondered.

My soul still ached to do a good fouetté. *Just one*, I thought, but I hesitated. The girl with the good extension repeated the combination across the floor, so I felt the green light to try a move of my own too. I went into my fouetté spin. The trouble was I couldn't stop. With all the stress of the move, I lost myself completely in the music in my head. I forgot where I was and who was watching. I thought back to my old class and went with it. I gave it all I had.

"Eight, nine . . . ," I counted, rotating fouettés ten times up and down on pointe, then two more times for good measure. I then hit a pose and checked myself in the mirror again. The pose wasn't good enough. The finger placement was wrong, but I hadn't completely lost my touch with the move. It had only been a week. I pretended again that it was like a vacation away, and it made me feel much better.

As I continued to examine my pose in the mirror, I noticed that some of the girls had moved back against the barre and were gawking at me. I realized I had done too much and immediately felt bad. The silence in the room was heavy. Ms. Oakland cleared her throat and clapped her hands.

"See you next week, girls!" she said, effectively ending the class. With the return to routine, the girls applauded. I clapped also, halfheartedly, and bent to take off my shoes.

"Your level is wrong for this class." I looked up in surprise to see Ms. Oakland standing over me, her mouth turned down. I stared at her for a second in shock and then walked off to the entryway to exchange my pointe shoes for sneakers. I then threw my pointe shoes in my bag with anger. What a rude teacher. This was definitely not the ballet school for me.

When I got to the car, Dad opened the door from inside, and I plopped down on the seat. Dad looked at me, warily taking in my expression.

"No? No good?"

"It's not my level. But thank you for trying." Petey kicked the back of my seat as the car took off, and I just stared out the window of the car the rest of the way home.

When we got home, I headed straight for my room. The workout in the ballet class had sent my endorphins soaring, despite the disappointment afterward, and I knew it was high time to give myself a good workout—in the only place available to me. I grabbed the new wooden barre and began with plié from first to fifth positions, and then stretched my legs on the bar, first right, then left. I did some super high battements to get my frustration out, and then held a coupé and pulled it up to passé, and inspected my form in the mirror. Restless, I still had to get rid of this boundless energy, and tour jeté'd twice, like a violent wind that swept through my room, but the violent wind was only me as I soared through the air. I tried a third jeté, but ran out of space, almost bumping into my bed again, but recovered, thankfully, without injury. Suddenly I heard my dad's voice echo down the hallway along with extra loud grunts from Petey. Oh, no. The pajama fight. I sighed as I realized, again, that my ballet would have to wait.

I walked down the hall to Petey's room, and saw them fighting. Like clockwork Petey refused to take off his red and green clothes to wear a brand-new set of blue print pajamas. Dad had won the first part of the battle; Petey stood on the bed in defense mode, in his underwear, like a football player anticipating the next play, but unsure of where to go. Dad, with little blue pajamas pants in one hand, tried to counter him but kept missing. Eventually Dad gave up.

"I'll do it, Dad," I offered and grabbed Petey. I tried to put the pj pants on him but he resisted even me. "Don't be so hard headed, Petey."

"They're new," Dad said.

"He hates them *because* they're new," I answered. Petey accidently kicked me in the tussle.

"Ow!" I let him go. Petey immediately put his red and green clothes back on and climbed into bed. He stared at us for a full minute and then closed his eyes to sleep. Dad and I looked at one another and shrugged.

"His new furniture comes next week."

"No!" I sat down on his little bed. "Send it back. It's too soon."

"The theme is trains. He *loves t*rains." It was true. Petey had train toys all over the place, but the new train bed would be unfamiliar. The new bed light with the caboose base already scared him.

"We'll have to stay with him every night until he or we fall asleep from exhaustion," I reminded him.

Dad put his head down for a moment, then sat down on the bed, tears forming in his eyes. "If your mother was alive, she'd know how to handle him. You have the same ability, Kendra. I am just butterfingered with him."

"No, you're not, Dad."

"I thought . . ." Dad said. "I thought that I'd have a son I could play ball with, take fishing. I didn't expect this." I put my hand on his shoulder. Dad looked beat. "Your mom," he said, wiping a tear away from his eye, "I miss her so much."

"Me too."

Memories of Mom came springing up through my soul, and I remembered us at the window in New York, staring at the lights. I could see her brown hair blowing in the breeze as we swung on the swings together in Central Park. I could hear her voice calling me from the kitchen in the apartment. I remembered then her wake and her funeral, that awful day, with everyone in black and I cried and cried. Thinking about Mom, I could almost smell her perfume that used to waft through the apartment. Moving away from the apartment made me feel like we moved away from Mom too, but I didn't say that to Dad. It wasn't the right time.

"She's always with us." Dad looked at me. "All around us, watching over us like an angel, I'm sure." At that moment, I envisioned Mom at the doorway to Petey's room, dressed in white with her flowing brown hair, looking ballerina-like with iridescent angel wings. I imagined her smiling.

"She was pretty," I said, remembering. "And I wanted to look just like her when I grew up." My imaginary mom at the doorway evaporated into thin air and reality came hit me hard.

"You do look like your mom, but you look like me too." Dad laughed a little. "Funny how one person can look like two," he said. "But Petey's a dead ringer for me." We both stared down at Petey, asleep in the bed. "We have to find a Regional Center. The insurance will pay for his aide for only another week." My head nodded automatically.

"I'll help any way I can," I said, and Dad kissed me on the head good night.

Guilt flooded me as he left Petey's room. Here I was complaining about a ballet school when my little brother's whole future could be at stake. Maybe I should consider Petey more and weigh the situation before I worry about my own. It's hard sometimes though . . . being perfect.

Chapter Six

The next morning, the kitchen smelled like pancakes, and its scent drew me in like a bear to a campsite. Dad looked silly. Wearing a chef's hat, he flipped a pancake high in the air, and it fell back down into the pan with flair. As I walked into the kitchen I hit the chair leg, stubbing my right toe.

"You okay?" Dad flipped the pancake again.

"Yeah." I sat down and held my head. "I just felt dizzy for a second."

"Stress of the move. We're all feeling it."

"I guess." The dizziness began to subside. "Maybe it's my low blood pressure." That must be it, I reasoned.

"And don't forget your circulation problem."

"My left leg does feel numb," I said, rubbing my leg. I had been numb on and off for about a year, usually if I sat too long. It hadn't bothered me that much until now.

"My mother had it," Dad continued, "and it often skips a generation, things like that. Vein circulation problem, baldness, diabetes . . ."

"Dad! I'm not going bald, and I'm not diabetic. The numbness—I felt it on the airplane."

"There you go. People often get it on airplanes. Nothing to worry about."

I looked over at Petey, who had already started on his breakfast, picking the pieces of the pancake up with his hands.

"Today you'll have to return home from school promptly to relieve the temporary aide and babysit Petey. I'm still looking for a school with van pickup and he still needs to be connected with a good regional center."

"Okay, Dad."

"Petey doesn't like the aide from the agency."

"Don't worry, Dad."

"I won't. You have a way with him, honey. I just hope it doesn't impact your social life at school."

"I don't belong to any clubs yet. I'm still looking for a dance school." I didn't have the heart to tell him that school held nothing for me but loneliness, the nickname "Opera Girl," and Future Farmers of America club.

Dad placed a cup of orange juice on the table in front of me. I gulped it down, ate one small pancake, then got up to leave. But I sat back down again, dizzy once more, and sneezed.

"You have a cold." Dad smiled, his white teeth matching his chef's hat and already nearly white hair. He offered me another pancake. I shook my head no but he continued. "The school's requirement for a whooping-cough shot might have given you some side effects." Dad smiled again reassuringly.

I headed out to the school bus, which just turned the corner.

What I didn't tell Dad was that my right leg had gone numb too.

❦

It wasn't until the beginning of the assembly at school when the numbness in my right leg finally subsided. Panic gripped my heart. What if the numbness happened when I danced? The thought really scared me. The circulation started up, and I promised myself I wouldn't sleep on my right side anymore to avoid my muscle going to sleep. My thoughts about my leg were broken by the noise of bored students in forced camaraderie all over the gym's ancient bleachers.

"Opera Girl," Bailey Adams whispered to her friends on the bleacher across from me. She glanced at me, and her words floated through the air in my direction. What was with her anyway? In the first place, I was a dancer, not a singer. Stupid Bailey just latched onto the stupid phrase and wouldn't give it up. Then I saw Sylvan sitting with her goth group and tried to wave, but she didn't see me.

I turned my attention back to the band, which came banging down the center of the gym at full blast.

"Go, Lions!"

The screams rang out as Bailey and her clones scurried down to the bottom of the bleachers and fell in line with the parade of instruments. The band tried too hard, playing a hip-hop version of "Stars and Stripes," as Bailey backflipped in front. The assembly, I realized, was a pep rally, designed to prep us for the homecoming game and the bonfire over the weekend.

Some guys booed the team as the players marched out in their gold football uniforms. The players waved them off, disgusted.

"Lions rule! Go, Lions!" A horde of voices screamed back at the disloyal guys, and the crowd clapped in response. I wished the whole event would hurry up. My tailbone hurt, and I felt a throb on my bony spine as the hard bleacher pressed into it. Bailey flipped again and landed, throwing her arms up into the air for applause.

"Go, Bailey!" The rowdy guys whistled and hooted.

The band sounds distorted in my ears as well, so I withdrew into myself. My mind went into my own world of familiar New York City sights and sounds, as if I wasn't even a part of this California cacophony.

I closed my eyes and breathed in the imaginary smell of New York—the steam rising from the manhole covers mingling with the aroma of fresh bagels; the smell of the streets mixing with garbage; exhaust from city buses synthesizing with the expensive perfume of the people passing by. I could walk for hours in New York by myself and never once feel lonely. Here in California you had to drive miles to see another person, and even in this crowded high school gym, I felt lonelier than I had ever been in my entire life. I was like an outsider, a foreigner in the land of sunny California. I might as well have been from Indonesia, for all they cared. To them, the East Coast was another planet where "opera girls" and ballerinas lived, ballerinas who stupidly wore prep school blazers with jeans to public school.

"Sorry!"

My memory dissolved like a PowerPoint animation slide as a trio of giggling girls chased by two guys crossed in front of me in the bleachers, almost falling into my lap. I pulled my legs up to allow them to pass, and they went on their giggling, screaming way.

Principal Biondi tapped the outdated microphone equipment down below and began to speak.

"We're outta here, man." The rowdy boys ran out of the bleachers before Principal Biondi could stop them. As they passed the cheerleaders down below, Bailey stopped one of the guys and whispered in his ear, pointing in my direction. The guy turned back toward the bleachers and yelled.

"Hey, Opera Girl!" He and the guys laughed and took off, but the rest of the gym looked directly up at me and stared. Several girls beside me ducked down low, not to be associated with me in this spotlight. My face froze and I thought I'd die from embarrassment as everyone, including Principal Biondi, gawked.

"That's enough," Biondi warned, and most everyone turned back toward him. Some students still snickered, and others repeated the name. "That's enough," the principal repeated. He looked annoyed, then changed his dynamics to an artificial, happy voice, announcing the fall schedule—football games, dances, holidays, midterms, spirit days, and so on. Grateful for the reprieve, I told myself to focus on something else. Petey. I could be strong for him. Thinking of my little brother, I tuned out for the rest of the assembly.

❧

I kept my head down low as I entered my next class, but was surprised when a pair of sneakers stopped in front of me. I looked up to see a couple of kids from my class standing there.

"Don't worry about those guys. They're idiots," said one girl. "They're just troublemakers. Don't mind them." I nodded, and a guy chimed in."Losers with a big L," he said, "and everyone knows Bailey instigated it too."

"Bailey's such a brat," another guy said. "It's a pity she's cute." He laughed, as did the other guys in the class, as if being cute somehow forgave meanness. I smiled a little, grateful for some camaraderie, but not all were convinced. Two girls still snickered nearby, one right next to me.

Just when I thought things couldn't get worse, they did.

Mr. Hoyt started up the class and asked a question.

"Martin Luther King's life had such a big impact on the history of our modern world. What was the impact of his death?"

Since I had just done my speech back at Madison School in New York on MLK, I was confident that I knew the answer. Still, I hesitated, wanting to stay obscure in the class. No one else seemed to know, so I wrote the answer down on a piece of paper and slipped it to one of the girls who had been nice to me. I didn't want to appear like a know-it-all.

The girl smiled but gave the paper back to me.

"Answer it. You know it," she whispered and smiled sweetly, so I tentatively put my hand up to answer the question.

"Martin Luther King gave the 'I Have a Dream' speech to inspire," I volunteered, "but it was actually his 'I've Been to the Mountaintop' speech that was the last one he ever gave. He was assassinated the next day. Because of that, it made people think and take more notice of the cause, especially since Mr. King promoted nonviolence and he died in such a violent way."

"And the next *Jeopardy* contestant is . . " The girl next to me said, and some of the students around us laughed. "I've got to text this to Bailey!" The girl grabbed her cell phone and typed until Mr. Hoyt pulled it out of her hand.

"Cell phones will be confiscated," he warned. He put it in his desk, then straightened his bow tie. The girl laughed again, whispering that she'd tell everyone after school. "It's so funny," she added.

I was supposed to pretend I was stupid, I guess. Stupid apparently won points for popularity.

Then the girl spilled her water bottle on me, not so accidentally.

"Oh, sorry!" she said, mopping it off the floor.

"No drinks in the classroom." The teacher was livid, but I was even madder. It went all over my jeans, making me look like the total nerd I now felt like.

As I sat there dripping with water, it reminded me of the time a girl threw up all over my social studies book in grade school. The girl just stood up and heaved all over my desk. I had to keep the smelly book all year with the pages on ancient Greece stuck together by old vomit, so I couldn't read it and failed the test. Now, instead of vomit, I wore someone else's backwashed water.

I thought about my too-thin arms and legs that were perfect for the Manhattan Dance, but now stuck out of my pale, yellow tee shirt and my ruined water-stained jeans in a public high school environment that seemed to have no culture. The blazer was already history, and I wore the worst-looking jeans I could find, but I still looked geeky. What was the use?

Should I have to change myself because others didn't like it? Couldn't I be me? Would I have to endure this torture all through high school? I wanted to shout back at the unkind kids that I was not the clown they thought I was, but it was better to keep quiet. If I spoke, anything I said could be held against me in the court of teenage rule. They'd only have more pleasure spreading the story about how Opera Girl got upset in class. No, it was better to remain silent, at least for now.

Chapter Seven

After school, I walked from the corner bus stop and found a silver Mercedes parked in our driveway next to my Dad's white Honda. Who was here? Entering, I tripped on the door jamb as Dad called me from the kitchen. He was wearing the chef's hat again.

"Kendra?" he called out again. I saw Petey in the rec room, rocking on Mom's old rocking chair and picked him up before heading to the kitchen. "On the table," Dad indicated, and I looked over to see dishes and napkins.

"Whose car is that outside?"

"Look at the table!" I looked. Dad set the plates, utensils, and napkins almost as nicely as Mom used to do. I held back a laugh when I noticed the napkins. Dad had clearly meant them to be swans, but they looked more like drooping turtles with long necks.

"Nice table, Dad."

"No! The keys!" Dad pointed to my seat at the table. Sure enough, there was a set of keys. Car keys. His car keys!

"You're letting me drive?" I put Petey down.

"Super Symmetry Computers gave me a company car. Executive perk." Dad beamed. "Once you change your New York license to a Californian one, it's all yours." I ran to the front door to see Dad's new silver Mercedes and my own precious, little, white Honda.

There was silence. I couldn't speak. I picked the keys up and examined them. Dad's keys. Would they somehow magically transform to mine this very night?

"Thanks, Dad." I squealed in joy and ran to him, giving him a big hug. He dropped two hardboiled eggs from the salad onto the floor in the process. "I've got wheels!" I squealed again, but Petey held his ears. I forgot for a moment that he hated noise. "Sorry, Petey," I said and kissed him on the top of the head, but Petey ran off.

"He'll be okay," Dad said. "Get your license." Dad's face registered mischievous joy as he picked up the smashed eggs.

"I'll get my license and drive in no time," I told him. "Awesome!"

"I'm sorry the ballet school we tried yesterday wasn't the one for you. But I thought with a car available, you could investigate ballet schools and find the one you want."

Petey returned to the kitchen, curious, and sat down at the table again as Dad put a chef salad down in front of us.

"I asked around for you. Apparently, this Napa Valley region has a lot of performing arts in the area. It's like a mini New York here—lots of culture, they say. They have a symphony, a ballet company, a theater . . ."

"Among the grapes?" I laughed a little as Dad ate one of the smashed eggs. If I had to lose my old ballet class, at least the car keys gave me hope. A good, elite-level dance class . . . I could find one now. I knew it.

☙❧

With license in hand and Dad in the passenger seat, I made my way through the acres of farmland. Dad leaned over and pointed to a spot on the map guide.

"You have GPS, but I want you to navigate. Remember, I signed the DMV papers for responsibility for your license."

"But it slows me down." I turned a corner with the map stretched out over my lap, the dashboard, and Dad's knees.

"Nevertheless, it's an important skill. What if we have a cyber attack and all the electronics go down?"

"That's an extreme example, Dad."

"Nevertheless . . ."

Dad could be such a parent sometimes. But I didn't care. I was driving around in my new, very middle-aged-looking, but very available white Honda.

"There it is." I pointed to another shopping center dance school. Toddlers exited with dance moms, and teens in various colored leotards, looking jazzy, held ballet slippers and dance bags.

"What do you think?" Dad asked, not encouraged himself.

"I dunno." Hesitating, I sized up the dance place. "It looks like another factory school." My heart deflated. I'd really wanted this to be the one, but it wasn't.

☙❧

A mile down the road, I found another small dance

studio, but it was too small. I looked in the window and the center wooden floor was the size of a CD cover. I walked back to the car where Dad waited with Petey, both of them eating a fast food burger.

"Not in the car!" I freaked out. "You'll drop crumbs!"

"You never worry about eating in my car," Dad protested.

"That's different," I said, but then realized he was right and I laughed. Dad handed me a small burger.

"We still have a deal, you know. You eat decently in exchange for the dance training." I shook my head and he chucked my cheek. "Enjoy."

I took the burger and actually ate it without stripping it clean of fatty dressing and cheese. Dad noticed and put his hand on my shoulder. "Boy, you are depressed." I didn't respond. I just ate and planned the route for the next potential dance school.

⟡

Down another road, I found the third one on my list.

"Go in and try it. We're right on time." I took my dance bag, tried the class, but returned empty-spirited.

"It's not bad, but this one's really far to drive, and it's Cecchetti-style ballet."

"What's the difference?"

I rolled my eyes.

"Different port de bras," I said. "It's beautiful to watch, but . . ." I stopped because Dad didn't understand what I meant, but my training was muscle memory and I could never comprehend those different arm positions. I was too entrenched in the Russian style.

"It is really far," Dad admitted, "and you are a new driver." I looked over my list.

"One more," I said, checking the last school on the Internet on my cell phone. "No!"

"What?"

"It's in the middle of mall?" I shook my head with regret. "Where's that Napa Valley dance company you heard about, Dad?"

"They didn't give me a name, hon. I'll get it tomorrow at work."

Napa Valley ballet had to have a school or at least a good recommendation for one. Was there a ballet school somewhere out there for me among all those grapes and vines?

Later that night, I checked my email for Miss Irina's response. There was nothing. Again. My eyes lowered and my heart sank. She was probably away, I told myself. Sometimes she went out to the Hamptons, just like I told Dad. He didn't believe it, but I had to believe it. I would believe it. Yes, she had to be at the beach in the Hamptons. That's why I hadn't heard from her.

My eyes went straight from the computer to my pointe shoes on the bed beside me. The toe caps lay separately next to the pink, satin shoes, with remnants of bloodstains inside them. Practicing in my bedroom wasn't the same as class. Ballet was a group activity. I needed the music. I needed the teacher. I needed Miss Irina.

I threw the thoughts of Miss Irina out of my mind and stretched on the floor with my computer beside me. I started writing an email to Liz. Just thinking of writing to Liz made me feel like I was back in New York again, waiting to take class. My frustration poured out of my fingertips as I typed Liz's name into the chat program at Manhattan Dance's website.

"It's a tundra out here," I wrote. I needed Liz and others to weigh in on my situation.

"Hi," Liz's reply came immediately, despite the time difference.

SWAN KENDRA: Seriously though. It's a wasteland. I'm in total New York withdrawal. Feel like I'll die if I don't take Miss Irina's class in the next minute!

GISELLE LIZ: Calm down!

SWAN KENDRA: There isn't a decent dance school this side of the Mississippi.

GISELLE LIZ: How 'bout Los Angeles?

SWAN KENDRA: . . . . if I lived in LA!

GISELLE LIZ: Right . . . What's the nearest city?

SWAN KENDRA: Apple Glen.

GISELLE LIZ: You're kidding. Where u living . . . in deep south?

SWAN KENDRA: It's not funny. My life's over!

GISELLE LIZ: Okay. What's the nearest BIG city?

SWAN KENDRA: San Francisco or LA . . . but it's miles and miles!

GISELLE LIZ: Go to the Bay Ballet.

SWAN KENDRA: My life is over!

AURORA 35: What about a Los Angeles Ballet school?

A flood of comments came in, and they all said the same thing.

JULIET 1208: Go to LA!

ODETTE: Los Angeles Ballet!

CORSAIR GUY: Los Angeles, girl!

CLARA 537: Go to Los Angeles Good schools!

SYLPHIDE 19: Go to LA . . . Kiss Petrov for me. :)

SWAN KENDRA: I don't know if I can. My life is over . . .

GISELLE LIZ: Since it's over, I might as well tell you. They picked Sara Harrington for the snowflake part in the *The Nutcracker.* Sorry. Check her Facebook. Here's the link . . .

I clicked on Sara's Facebook link to see my ballet competitor in the photos online. Sara Harrington looked happy, a huge smile on her face. Why not? After all, she was a snowflake.

SWAN KENDRA: Gotta go.

I closed the computer and laid my head on the pillow. As the music of *The Nutcracker* floated into my head, I felt my heart throb, but I wasn't going to cry, no matter what. My heart continued throbbing since I had no control over that, but I held back the tears as I thought about the snowflake, Miss Irina's missing email, and my miserable life. But then my Spartan spirit kicked back up again. I shot up in bed.

The girls were right! I could check out Los Angeles for ballet or drive to San Francisco. Just because it was far away didn't mean it wasn't an option. I grabbed my white laptop and carefully mapped the distance and the route to San Francisco. I wasn't going to wait for life to happen to me anymore. I wanted to make my mark on it. Succeed or fail, I was going to San Francisco to take a class. I had a car now. I researched the times on the site and couldn't wait for my life to go back to some sort of normal. I wasn't sure when I'd go, but I knew I had to find a way.

With the TV remote, I clicked on one of my taped movies. The music of the film *The Red Shoes* played, and I felt comfort surround me.

"Nothing will deter me from my goal," I said and settled in to watch the movie for the umpteenth time.

Chapter Eight

Riding the school bus home the next day, I reached for some flyers in my backpack. I'd gathered them from the school club activity day. I was taking Dad's advice to join a club in an effort to get my mind off my moving woes. I wanted to join a club about as much as I wanted to step on a bed of nails, but I'd promised, so I looked at the flyers.

"French Club," I whispered as the bus hit a bumpy section of road. Nice if I took French. Only I didn't. Latin Club . . . I did take Latin. Dad forced me to continue the prep program from my New York school so I got stuck with Latin II. Kids who joined the Latin Club at Seneca High were labeled geeks for life. Latin club was out. Math and Science Club . . . No. I'd always been hopeless at math.

I looked at another flyer. It was the *Seneca 'Zine*. They were looking for writers and columnists. I liked writing. I got A's in English. I'd written some stories before. Journalism . . . hmm. I decided to tell Dad that I would try it if they'd take me.

A bump in the road almost threw me out of my seat. Surprised, I looked up to find the cause.

"Manure! Ugh." I stared out the window at the bags of spilled manure on the road that must have fallen from a passing truck. I realized that we'd just driven through it all, and the smell caused everyone to close the windows of the bus. I heard slam after slam of the windows, but one boy's window got stuck.

"Close it, nerd!"

"Hurry!"

"Hey, it's just manure." Three guys laughed and helped the nerd push the window up, but when they shoved it too hard, it got even more stuck. It was too late anyway. The odor permeated the inside of the bus, sticking to our clothes, and I just wanted to gag.

After I gathered my things again from the floor, I sat back and stared out the window of the school bus, which stopped again. We dropped off passengers at this stop every day. The girl with the scooped nails and the blond bully got off and walked the long road up to a farmhouse. As the bus took off, I watched them. That's when I saw the sign.

"Academy of the Fields—Dance School." I had to refocus my eyes. Did that sign say "Dance School?" I turned sharply to look at the sign as we drove away. The letters were unmistakable. It was a dance school, somewhere up that long, long road to the farmhouse. As I stared at a smaller building nearby in the midst of the vineyard, the girl and guy from the bus walked into the small building, then the bus rounded a corner and I lost sight of the whole scene.

Were the girl and the blond bully both dancers? Was that why the freshman kid made fun of the cute blond guy that first day on the bus? I wondered whether he really was a bully or if he just had to defend himself that day.

My curiosity got the better of me and I whipped out my cell phone and searched for the Academy of the Fields. There it was. Its website appeared to me on screen like a magic wish that had just been granted. I couldn't read the words well on the bumpy bus, so when I got home, I dashed to the computer. Petey climbed the stairs to my room after me.

"Not now, Petey," I told him. Petey sat down on the bed and rocked a little with his legs drawn up. I decided to let him stay because he was so quiet. I returned my attention to the website.

"How did I miss this one?" I muttered. I saw a photo of girls in black leotards, pink tights, and pointe shoes taking class at the barre.

"It looks professional," I whispered. I clicked to look at the schedule. They had advanced level ballet, pointe, pas de deux, and adagio starting at three in the afternoon every day! I could hardly catch my breath. The rest of the photos on the site showed no annual recital, no tots, and classes on Saturdays. And there was something about a ballet company . . . This might be a real school. Their motto was "For the serious minded student." A footnote on the website said "By audition only." I grabbed my cell phone and called the number.

The next day after school, I put Petey in the car and, with my New York license now a Californian one, I headed to ballet. The director of the school, Mrs. Cassidy, told me on the phone to take an advanced class and she would assess me. I was sure that there would be no problem, but I still felt nervous. I hadn't taken a real ballet class since we left New York three weeks ago. My muscles were turning to jelly. That's what I feared most—jelly muscles.

I turned into the long road leading up to the ballet school nestled in the middle of a vineyard, of all things! I admit it, I was getting desperate. I needed class to keep up my elite training in order to go back to New York to audition for the company. My snowflake part had slipped away to Sara Harrington; my ballet career could slip away, too, if I didn't get these jelly legs back into shape.

I stopped the car in the dirt driveway of the school, with the vineyards in back of me. I held on to the steering wheel and just stared at the building. A sign that arched over the door of a fairy tale–like cottage read, "Academy of the Fields Dance." It was like seeing a vision rise up in the middle of the farm. I half expected a halo to surround the dance school, but then Petey grunted and broke my daydream.

Inside the one-story school, I held Petey's hand tightly and approached a girl at the desk near the entrance. I asked for a schedule, which the girl gave to me. I recognized her. She was the scooped-nail girl from the bus.

"I know you," the girl said and smiled. "I'm Becca."

"Kendra," I returned. "How are your scooped nails?"

Becca laughed.

An older woman also laughed as she approached. "She thinks she has the disease of the week." She was attractive with short, sandy-blonde hair. "I told you to stop watching those TV medical shows."

Becca turned to her. "I can't. The guy on the show is so cute."

The woman laughed again.

"Mom, this is Kendra from school." Becca turned to me again. "And this is?"

"My brother, Petey."

"Hi, Petey," Becca said, but my brother didn't respond.

"He's just here to watch. He'll be good."

Becca shrugged. "This is my mother," she said. "She runs the school."

"I'm Mrs. Cassidy." The woman extended her hand and shook mine. Seeing Mrs. Cassidy was like gazing at an angel. I could see photos on the wall behind her—Mrs. Cassidy at a younger age dancing ballet with the Joffrey and at the Harkness. The immense relief that floated over my being caused me to crumble.

I started to blurt out my situation, the whole story about the move, the lack of class. I ended up sobbing in the entrance to the school and cried extra hard about the snowflake part. I poured my heart out until Mrs. Cassidy put her arm around me. Petey touched my leg, and I stopped crying, not wanting to upset him.

"You were really in line for the apprentice program?" Mrs. Cassidy glanced over at her own photos of youth in ballet companies and turned back to me. She smiled. She understood. I could tell. She was the first one who understood since I left New York. This lady knew what it meant to lose your standing in the apprentice program or to lose the part of a snowflake in *The Nutcracker.*

"Let's begin class," Mrs. Cassidy said. She clapped her hands and showed me the way to the barre. I put Petey in the corner on a folding chair, and he sat motionless. He had never seen a ballet class.

As I grabbed the barre along the wall, I saw Bailey Adams on the portable barre in the center. She looked at me like I was from Mars. Mrs. Cassidy clapped, and I turned my attention back to class.

I followed Mrs. Cassidy's instruction in the barre work, fell in with the music. We started with pliés. We progressed from tendues to rond de jambe, frappés, and through to grand battements. My muscles were tight and felt a little numb. The time between classes did make me a little out of shape. I stopped to tie my pointe shoes for the center and saw Mrs. Cassidy eye me as I did the combination. It sounded silly in the middle of a vineyard ballet school, but I wanted to impress Mrs. Cassidy. I don't know why. Even though I had been a student at Manhattan Dance, for some reason, I wanted Mrs. Cassidy to like me.

I held out my long, willowy arms and did arabesque. I posed and held it on pointe for five seconds. I counted it and felt surprised that I hadn't lost much extension. I began the fouettés and did ten but noticed from my peripheral vision that everyone else had stopped. I kept going, though, and heard the count.

"Eleven, twelve, thirteen . . ."

From the corner of my eye, I saw Bailey Adams staring at me with her mouth agape. I also noticed the blond bully lean against the wall, and I watched him again on the next spin of the fouetté. I also saw, between turns, Bailey smiling at the cute, blond guy, but he ignored her and looked at me. I recognized his sandy-haired stance. It was him—the one who threw the backpack that first day on the school bus.

I turned my head and spun, then turned my head back. I caught his glance on every turn and watched him stare at me. He had a handsome face with an errant lock of hair that fell over one eye, like the perennial bad boy in the movies. His mouth, though, soon turned into a sly smile. He had to be Mrs. Cassidy's son, I realized, because he looked just like her.

Catching me staring at him, he widened his smile, but I wasn't sure I liked the way he looked at me.

"Fourteen . . . fifteen . . . sixteen . . ."

I came down from the fouettés and struck a pose in fourth position, then glanced over at Mrs. Cassidy, who smiled with approval.

"Let the training begin," she said. I beamed with delight, then looked around for Petey. Between the fouettés and the cocky guy, I'd forgotten all about my brother. He wasn't on his chair. I panicked. Looking around the room, I found him sitting near a wall. Several ballet skirts hung from hooks nearby, and Petey had taken one of the skirts. He sat in another corner of the room with a pink tutu on his head like it was normal.

Horror filled my soul as I thought I'd get in trouble, but the others laughed at his cuteness. Relieved, I laughed too, just like everyone else.

❦

At dinnertime, I ate steak and salad heartily as Dad looked on in approval.

"Kendra, I haven't seen you eat like that since you were back in—"

"New York?" I interrupted him and smiled. "Well, I found my own little New York."

"Tell me." Dad took a big bite of steak. Excited, between big forkfuls of steak and salad myself, I blurted it out.

"I took Petey to a new ballet studio today. I think I've found it." I pointed my fork at Dad for emphasis. "*The* one!" Dad sighed with relief. "And it's in the middle of a vineyard with a pumpkin patch too. Can you believe it?"

Dad laughed. "Oh, Kendra . . . you might just turn into a farm girl yet." He chuckled, and I tossed a piece of lettuce at him. Petey, who had been silent at the table in his usual red-and-green clothes, suddenly grunted.

෴

Every day after that, I drove up with Petey after school to the Academy of the Fields. Petey sat in his usual corner with a pink practice ballet skirt for comfort. It really surprised me that from the very first moment, he never once showed fear or confusion at the class. Mrs. Cassidy said she thought he liked the piano music. I thought he liked the movement. Sometimes Petey would throw his legs around or raise an arm in imitation. He was watching, cognizant. I knew it.

After the barre and center floor work, I asked Becca to watch Petey for me while I got changed, and he stayed with her without complaint. When I came out of the ladies room, I saw Petey looking at the ballet barre.

"You're really good," Becca said. It was an honest

comment. I could tell she really meant it as she scratched her blonde hair in amazement. "Your New York training comes through." She smiled with her crinkly pug nose covered with freckles and a dimple in both of her cheeks.

"The others are not chopped liver, either," I commented, looking at a few girls still stretching at the barre in class. "They're pretty good."

"This is a serious school," Mrs. Cassidy said, walking up to us from behind.

"You're right," I said as I rubbed my sore muscles. I looked a little closer at the photos on the wall near the front desk. There was a picture of the girls in my class in costume. It looked like the ballet *Coppélia*.

"We don't do recitals, but we do a semi-annual performance. We have a small ballet company and perform at the Cultural Arts Festival of Napa Valley." I looked at the photos again.

This was the ballet company that Dad talked about. He was right after all. As I perused the photos again on the wall, I saw Becca and her bully brother. I pointed to him in the picture.

"That's Troy," Mrs. Cassidy said. "My son." I figured.

"He's varsity track and field at school but does ballet," Becca stated.

"Used to do ballet," Troy corrected her as he came into the room with bravado and held up a dramatic port de bras. He turned, then fell to his knees in a pose.

"He still does do ballet." Becca moved closer to me. "He partners with us in the shows and sometimes in class."

"Only to be near the pretty girls," Troy stated and gave that sly smile that he threw at me the very first day.

"The guys at school used to harass him all the time about it."

"And sometimes still do," he added with annoyance, "which is why I'm now their best track athlete."

"Yeah, now he's a god."

"Hey! They say it, not me." Troy posed again, this time like a statue, until Mrs. Cassidy hit him with a small towel.

"Stop showing off for Kendra." Troy bowed like a dancer.

"Sorry, but I don't do ballet anymore." Troy looked back at Becca and me, but mostly at me, I noticed.

"This is Kendra."

"Kendra, that's her name." Troy smiled.

"Don't mind him," Becca said. "He thinks he's Brad Pitt."

"I'm better than Brad Pitt. Don't forget I'm an Olympian god." Troy pinched Becca's cheek, and she smacked him.

"Just because every girl in school wants to go out with you doesn't mean you're a god," Becca shot back. "My brother's a little conceited."

"You're just jealous 'cause I went out with a girl whose brother you'd like to date." Becca winced at this.

"I'm a ballerina," Becca stated proudly. "I don't have time to date." I nodded in agreement. Besides, who'd want to date this obnoxious Olympian god anyway, no matter how cute?

"Well, I'm not a dancer anymore, so I have plenty of time to find babes." Babes? The word turned me completely off.

"You'll be at the rehearsals for the annual show, don't forget." Mrs. Cassidy tapped Troy on his shoulder. "So don't go too far up into those clouds, Thor."

Troy grabbed an apple from the basket on the front

desk, threw it up into the air, caught it, and took a large bite. "Ah, food of the gods." That was something I had to say about Troy. He was dramatic and meant for performance. He was several inches taller than Becca, but looked just like her. In fact, the whole family looked alike with sandy-blond hair, small noses, and fair Irish skin.

"We'll be auditioning for the spring performance in January," Mrs. Cassidy said and sat down at the desk.

Becca chose an apple and offered one to Petey, who took it, but he just stared at it.

"You can eat it," Troy said and made a gesture that Petey was crazy.

"Hey, you can bully kids on the bus but not my brother. Don't talk to him like that." Now I really didn't like Troy. No one messed with Petey.

"He's just standing there looking at the apple like an idiot."

"He's not an idiot," I said, gulping, then lowered my voice. "He's autistic." Troy's face dropped as he realized he'd said the wrong thing.

"I'm sorry." Troy hit his head with his hand like he was an idiot himself. For a moment, I felt that Troy might have really meant it, but I hated him for being mean to Petey.

"What's all this about bullying kids on the bus, Troy?" Mrs. Cassidy looked concerned, and I felt a little guilty for sounding like a tattletale.

"It's nothing, Mom," Becca covered for him. "Some kid made comments about Troy's virility because he does ballet. That's all."

"Used to do ballet!" Troy looked really irritated now.

Petey grunted, looked up at Troy, and squinted one eye,

like he always did when he thought something was funny. He never laughed, but he squinted his right eye, and I'd swear it was his way of laughing. Petey studied Troy for another moment, then took a big bite out of the apple, just like Troy did. Troy noticed and it threw him off balance for a moment. I broke the odd silence and asked Mrs. Cassidy about another picture on the wall.

"This one's from the Harkness Ballet," she stated. "Oh, the Harkness . . . they had the most beautiful practice rooms with hardwood floors and chandeliers." Mrs. Cassidy's eyes looked off in fond memory. "You felt as though you were dancing in the ballroom of a king." She sighed. "And here's another on tour with the Joffrey Ballet . . ." I was impressed. Mrs. Cassidy was the real deal, not like that awful Ms. Oakman at the boom-box recital factory.

"Would you want to hang out on the weekend, see a movie or something with Troy and me?" Becca posed the question, but my eyes went immediately toward Troy—Troy, the hot guy, who just happened to be Becca's brother, the Olympian god who somehow made me feel nervous with his overconfident attitude, the cute guy with a sandy lock of hair over one eye, which he pushed back like a model in a hot hair commercial. "Do you want to go on Saturday?" I realized that Becca was waiting for an answer.

"Yes," I said. "I'd love to go." I glanced over at Petey, sitting in his usual corner of the ballet room again, eating his apple and rocking quietly to the music of the sound system. He seemed lost in the music.

I hated to interrupt his daydream, whatever it was, but it was time to say good-bye and leave. I grabbed his little hand and led him out to the car. Becca followed us. Troy followed us outside too and grabbed me gently by the arm.

"Peace offering," Troy said. "Do you want some pumpkins? They're ripe to pick."

"And we've got hundreds of them," Becca added.

"Take them, please!" Troy said. I looked over at the large pumpkin patch in the back of the house. It overflowed. The plants were too crowded together in their fight for survival in the soil. Suddenly an idea hit me.

I grabbed Petey's hand tighter, and we all walked over to the patch of orange gourds. The orange streaked the field far behind the backyard. It seemed to stretch on for miles. As we approached the pumpkins, I pointed them out to Petey. There were large pumpkins; small, funny, white ones; red, short, round ones; and tall, oddly-shaped ones. Beyond the pumpkin patch I could see the acres of grapevines, tall with ripe fruit hanging and dragging the vines down.

"A Cinderella," Becca said. "For you." She picked off and placed a good-sized pumpkin on the ground beside me. I tried to get Petey to react and encouraged him to walk among a large patch of pumpkin plants, but he was too shy and wouldn't budge. We all watched him for a few minutes as he stared. He then circled around, waved his arms, then stopped dead, and stared again.

Mrs. Cassidy came out.

"Good, you're getting rid of some of these pumpkins."

"Why don't you sell them?" I asked. Mrs. Cassidy looked around at the plethora of gourds before us.

"We set up a stand on the weekends, but we have too many this year and too little help."

"I'd come over on the weekend to help you sell them at the stand," I volunteered.

"That'd be great," Mrs. Cassidy stated. She shook her head and laughed. "That would give me more time to do some of the ballet paperwork. I can't pay you, but I could give you one of your lessons free," she offered.

"That's okay. It would be fun to help out at the stand. I've never done anything like that before in New York."

"Good! Besides, I have to tend our main crop which supports us all—the vineyard."

"You do all this yourself?" I looked again at the vineyard, which started a few feet from the pumpkins. The rows of grapes looked so perfect that they almost seemed unreal.

"It's a small vineyard." Mrs. Cassidy sighed. "You see, when we moved here, I wanted a ballet school and Mr. Cassidy wanted a vineyard. We started both, but after Mr. Cassidy passed away, the job got too big for me alone. I hire help for the heavy work, and Troy helps me too." Mrs. Cassidy waved and walked inside the house. Troy picked up a shovel.

"I see that gods have to farm too." I laughed a little.

"Olympians shouldn't have to do this menial stuff. It takes too much time," Troy said, annoyed.

"Why don't you just use your thunderbolt to clear the field?" Becca teased. Troy punched her lightly on the arm. It was obvious that the two of them fought a lot but were still close.

Becca put two more pumpkins into the back seat of my car while Troy dug up another big pumpkin.

"Wait," I protested. "I only need one."

"You can line your porch with a family of jack-o'-lanterns."

Becca handed a tiny pumpkin to Petey, but he only stared at it as if he'd never seen one before up close. He stared at the orange color intently, just as he had stared at the red of the apple a few minutes before. He dropped his apple on the ground and touched a pumpkin, then retracted his hand.

I then picked Petey up and ran with him through the fields, being careful not to trip on the long vines that connected them. I stopped and swung Petey around and around in the middle of the pumpkin patch, and his right eye squinted a lot. As we spun, his hair blew in the breeze and we both felt free.

Putting Petey back down again, I grabbed his hand and we ran into the swatch of orange once more. We were having fun, fun in the field I saw every day from the school bus, back and forth on my way to Seneca High. Funny I rarely even noticed the pumpkin field, funny how you can see people and things every day, and never notice them at all until they mean something to you.

"Here's a good one." Troy approached and held a pumpkin, perfect and round. "Catch!" Surprisingly, he didn't throw it to me, but walked over to hand it to me instead. The trouble was that he lingered for a moment and stared right into my eyes. It was almost as if he could see into my inner being, and it made me nervous again.

As I looked up into his hazel eyes, I could feel his eyes searching me. *Oh, no, Thor*, I thought. *I'm not one of your Olympian maidens swooning at your feet.* I looked away, bothered that he still held the pumpkin, like a game of cat and mouse. Troy finally gave me the pumpkin, and it only irritated me further as his hand touched mine in the transfer. *Not working*, I thought. "Thanks," I stated, very matter-of-fact, and looked over at Becca, who was unaware of our little exchange.

Becca approached and swung Petey around near the edge of the field, but he ran back to me and withdrew again.

"He was fine with me before," Becca said, surprised. I just shrugged.

"He's moody." I held him for a moment, knowing that it wasn't just moodiness. He lived in an inner world all of his own.

Petey needed his bath at a certain time in the evening—seven o'clock. If delayed, it would be the witching hour, and Petey would be thrown off. He had to eat at seven in the morning, noon, and five in the evening, regardless of whether the rest of us ate with him. And he needed to wear only red or green.

Petey could be overstimulated easily and go into a small tantrum, and sometimes he would throw up unexpectedly when food didn't agree with him. I knew certain foods would bother him one week and not the next, if he would eat at all. And he always had to have his crackers. No, it wasn't moodiness. It was just my brother, Petey.

I sat Petey on top of an enormous, prize-winning gourd with a blue ribbon and a gold seal. We all said how cute he looked, but Petey just sat there with a blank look on his face. Wondering at that moment if my brother would ever react to anything in life, I felt fear grip my heart and again I worried about his future.

On Saturday morning, the pumpkin stand was busy when I arrived. Halloween was only a few days away, and business boomed for the various gourds on the fruit stand, as though it was a free giveaway at the mall. Several cars stopped and piles of kids pointed out the perfect pumpkin for their Halloween porches.

Becca and Troy sat at the stand on tall stools, taking in money and stashing it in a little metal box. I watched them as I parked my car on the dirt road. Along with the pumpkins, there were baskets of tiny grape bunches also being sold for good measure. As I approached the stand, Becca greeted me.

"Hey, sleepyhead."

"It's nine o'clock on a Saturday. I'm up early!" I walked toward the stand.

"You're a farmer now," Troy said. "Gotta keep farmer's hours."

"Do you take American Express?" a businessman interrupted us.

"Cash only," Troy answered and the man left in his silver Mercedes.

"Does that mean I have to go to bed by sunset too?" I asked.

Troy laughed this time as Becca tied an apron around my waist.

"Pumpkins will ruin designer jeans," Becca warned. I realized then that I had worn the wrong thing again. Why did I always do that? Overdressing in California seemed to be my downfall, and I didn't know how to fix it.

"How much for the big one?" A mother with a slew of kids pointed to the prize-winning gourd.

"Fifty dollars," Troy answered.

"That's a lot," she commented.

"It won in the fair," he insisted. "It'll be the hit of your party."

"I'd rather spend it on a caterer," the woman said.

"No one will have one like it," Troy returned, and the woman's eyes widened.

"I'll take it." Troy's salesmanship—no, his godlike status—mesmerized the woman, and it took me by surprise too. He was good.

The stand was crowded and crazy like that all day, and even though my legs ached from standing, and my back ached from bending over picking up pumpkins and putting them down again when the sale failed, I had fun talking to Becca and Troy as we took in the cash.

Mrs. Cassidy brought us lunch and iced tea while we sold our gourds, and the sun's shadow moved from left to right faster than we realized. It was already four o'clock in the afternoon. The cars dwindled along the road, so we packed up the rest of the pumpkins in a little pickup truck and drove back to the house.

"You're now officially a farmer," Troy said as he drove, and I bonked him on the head with a baby pumpkin in protest.

"Three hundred dollars today!" Mrs. Cassidy smiled as she collected the money at the house and doled some of the pumpkin money out to us. "For the movie tonight," she said and handed it to Becca.

"Thanks," I replied and eyed Mrs. Cassidy. "I've never seen you like this before."

Elegant Mrs. Cassidy, the former Joffrey ballet dancer, stood in front of us with a smudge of dirt on her face, wearing old overalls and sneakers. She had a spade in her pocket, obviously having worked in the soil.

"We're harvesting the grapes." I looked up to see some men and women walking from the fields. "My neighbors. We help each other out."

"Wanna see the vineyard?" Becca took me by the arm, and Mrs. Cassidy and Troy followed. I could see some of the rows of grapes ahead of me, knocked down. There was a large truck filled with bunches of green and purple grapes ready to go somewhere.

"What do you do with all the grapes?" I was such a city girl.

"We sell them to a winery," Mrs. Cassidy answered. "We have our own label, *Academy of the Fields*.

"Just like the ballet school?"

Mrs. Cassidy nodded. "Here, take some grapes home." Becca handed me a basket of extras from the harvest. I tasted one, and its juice burst in my mouth.

"They're delicious."

"Watch the stems," Troy added.

"Not officially grapes for eating, but they're good anyway." Mrs. Cassidy laughed as I looked at the grapes in the basket. I then saw the grapevines left in the field.

Each vine wound around a tall steel or wooden stake. There was wire over the top to catch the vines. The leaves were large, edging over the grapes like a shelter for the tiny purple fruit.

"It smells so good," I said, breathing in the aroma. "It's a strange mixture, like grapes, foliage, and . . ." I tried to think of the right word. ". . . earth."

"You're a farmer." Becca and Troy said it at the same time and laughed.

"No! I'm a New York City ballet dancer," I protested, but ended up laughing too.

❧

Even though we were all tired from selling pumpkins, Becca and Troy offered to pick me up later that night for the movie. They drove up to our house in their mom's car.

"They're here, Dad." I put on more lip gloss in the entry-way hall mirror.

"Okay, hon. Have a good time," he called out.

"I will," I said and brought Petey into the kitchen. Dad sat at the table with his usual ice cream after dinner. Kissing Petey, I headed for the door, but Petey ran after me. He grunted a few times. "No, Petey. You have to stay here."

"Uh . . . ," Petey grunted again. He put one arm up above his head and left it there, hanging in the air. I put his arm down again and brought him back to the kitchen, but he ran after me again. Dad got up to get him and grabbed his hand, but Petey broke the grasp. "Uh . . . ," he said again and put his arm up in the air in port de bras. I put his arm down once more and bent to eye level to speak to him.

"I gotta go, Petey, but I'll be back." Petey threw himself on the floor and kicked and screamed. The shrieks were embarrassingly loud. The cutest boy I ever saw, who was also a ballet dancer and an Olympian god, was getting out of his mom's blue car to come to my door, and my brother was throwing a tantrum.

I loved Petey, but at that moment, I wanted to disown him.

Troy came to the door and stared, and I almost died. "I'm just going to the movies, Petey."

Petey continued to scream at the top of his lungs, and

embarrassed, I had had it. I picked him up off the floor and shouted. "Stop it!"

Petey's face went blank. When I saw his little face, my guilt crashed down on me for even thinking of yelling at him or disowning Petey. How could I have thought something like that? Was I just a self-centered, selfish person? "Maybe I should stay with him," I volunteered.

"Go. I'll take care of him," Dad commanded, so I took advantage of the moment.

"Don't forget to change his red-and-green pajamas," I said, reaching for the door.

"He's been wearing them for a week."

"For your Dad," Troy said, and he handed me a bottle of *Academy of the Fields* champagne. "My mom sent it over." Dad took the bottle, inspected the label, and then smiled. Troy nodded, unsure how to act in this odd domestic melee.

"Tell your mom thanks for me," Dad said. Petey calmed down, and Dad made him wave good-bye.

As we went to the car, I realized that Troy hadn't said anything disparaging about Petey's behavior at all.

Chapter Nine

We arrived at the movies and found a really long line. Troy volunteered to get us burgers at a restaurant across the street. He brought the food back to the movie line, where we all ate standing up.

"What happened to Petey?" Troy asked.

"He's autistic," I told him. "He's very sweet—"

"I know," Becca interrupted.

"But he can have wicked temper tantrums." I took a slice of unmelted cheese off my burger and threw away one of the buns. I folded the remainder and took another bite of my reduced burger. "Too many carbs." Becca and Troy understood.

"Oh no!"

Troy snickered as Becca inspected her arm closely. "What's the matter this time?"

"It's a rash." She looked up. "*The* rash," she said.

"It's allergies." Troy seemed annoyed now.

"On the TV show last night," Becca continued without missing a beat, "a middle-aged man got a rash and he didn't know that it was related to cancer, so he ignored it thinking it was"—Becca looked at Troy—"an allergy." She looked back to me. "And then he died."

"What?" I laughed now. "That sounds stupid!"

"No." Becca was serious. "It was based on fact."

"You're crazy," Troy said. "You know that, don't ya?" He then turned to me. "Tell us about New York."

"I dunno. It's too soon."

"Come on . . . Tell us. Becca wants to be in a company someday and I'd like to live there too. Tell us what to expect."

"Yeah," Becca echoed. "Tell us." I wanted to talk about New York. I loved New York. But the thought of it made me too sad. Becca and Troy seemed really interested, though, so I poured my heart out about my favorite city.

I told them about the restaurants, where takeout was king, and about the shopping and the Broadway shows. I told them how at night New York looked like a giant sparkling jewel, and how in the day Central Park was a beautiful oasis of green with a large lake and a gazebo to sit in to watch the little boats go by. Little frogs in the lake would poke their noses up through the muddy water to greet you, and ducks would catch crumbs from your hot dog bun. I told them about ice skating and the angels at Rockefeller Center at Christmas, the hansom cabs at Fifty-ninth Street, and the Village, where you could browse through great old bookstores and interesting shops to buy one-of-a-kind clothes.

As we moved up in the movie line, I told them about the street fairs in New York on different avenues, Jones Beach in the summer, and how the snow would stop the buses sometimes in the winter, but never the subways. These never stopped, snow or not.

I told them about a previous blackout, and how the elevator wouldn't work and we had to climb fourteen floors to our apartment with flashlights to see in the dark.

I warned them about the smell of the street from the exhaust of buses, the intense humidity in the summer, and the wicked thunderstorms that lit up the skyscrapers like daylight. I told them about my secret place for lunch in a little space between two buildings where there was a waterfall with tables and chairs to sit and enjoy the afternoon in the shade of honeysuckle trees right in the middle of Manhattan.

I told them about a fight at the elevator at a big department store at Christmas time, and how two men punched each other out to get into the elevator car until the store Santa came by to try to stop them, and the guards ran up to arrest them. And all the time Becca and Troy laughed at my stories.

"Yeah, well, I heard New York has bugs." Troy made a face.

"That's the bad part." I made a face too and laughed.

"But the ballet," Becca said. "What about the ballet schools?" My laughter now faded as I remembered.

"I used to see Andrei Voltaskaya take class every day." My voice slowed and I choked back a tear. "And Alyssa Trent too." My smile faded, and I put my head down. "My friend Liz and I used to watch the company, and I saw all of the mistakes as well as the beauty. I saw the company perspire from repeating the moves, and heard the complaining when they missed them. But I also saw the joy when it all worked in the practice room without the orchestra to make the ballet soar.

"And then it would be our turn again the next day. We would take class on the same floorboards that the ballet stars danced on the day before. The finalists for *The Nutcracker* hung on the bulletin board outside class, and we all gathered around it every time the list was cut down to eliminate. My name was still on the list . . . and so was Sara's . . ."

Becca put her arm around my shoulders. "And we know what happened . . ."

I put my arm around Becca in return. "I'm so glad that I found you both." Tears rolled down my eyes. Despite my pumpkin-picking and grape-smelling day, I was still homesick.

"Don't cry, Kendra." Becca hugged me. "You audition for the company in the spring, and next year, when we're ready, Troy and I will come to New York and audition for the company too—"

"You'll audition. I'll be an actor," Troy stated. "No ballet."

"Okay, no ballet for you," Becca said, "but we'll be there in New York together—all three of us. Deal?"

I laughed through my teary eyes. Suddenly, I felt worlds better. I had a plan. Becca and Troy felt my pain. They found the solution. The movie line finally moved, and we headed in—together.

The pumpkin patches of October and November turned quickly into the poinsettias of the Christmas season. The pine tree was decorated. The large twelve-foot tree shone like a department store display out on the large front lawn of our country house on Bordeaux Lane. Ours was the only outside tree, since the housing development was still new, and no trees grew on anybody's property except nurslings, newly planted. We bought a potted tree large enough to rope to our car and then we planted it.

There were hundreds of Christmas lights strung around the tree. Each of the fat, old-fashioned bulbs glowed that special haze of red, blue, green, and yellow. The halo surrounded each orb of glass, holding the glow of the filament within, cloudy, ethereal. Night had already fallen, and the colored lights twirled around the pine like a ballerina in a symbiotic pirouette of evergreen and electricity.

"Really nicely done this year." Dad's voice startled me.

"We did it together," I answered just as Petey emerged from the house. His eyes reflected a look of recognition at the glowing bulbs on the pine, and he stood there with his mouth agape for a moment. He then looked underneath. Not finding anything, he circled the tree.

"He recognized Christmas," I blurted out. Dad saw it. Yes, Petey recognized Christmas. It was something that he hadn't done for years. Petey reached out and touched one of the red bulbs. Trying to stop him, I reached out to grab his hand. I pulled my hand back from Petey, though, realizing that the bulbs were really cool. Dad reached out to him too.

"Leave him alone," I said gently. "Let's see what he does." Petey cupped one of the fat red bulbs in his hand. He watched the glow inside his little fist, like a boy with a firefly caught on a summer's night. He peered at the light seeping between his fingers and held tightly onto his clutch.

He captured a piece of magic, the light of which was trying to reach him somewhere in his mental abyss. Petey looked at his other hand for comparison, then switched back to the fist that held a piece of Christmas light in its grasp.

Dad moved toward him as Petey continued to look at the bulb in wonder. Dad cupped his hand on a green bulb nearby and let Petey see the emerald-like glow in his own larger fist. Petey laughed. It was a small laugh, but it was there.

I moved forward and grabbed a yellow bulb and showed it to Petey, who watched intently. He saw the amber glow of yellow creeping through my fingers, and he gasped a little. Then he looked back to his own fist and laughed— well, he made a grunting sound and then squinted.

He stared at his fist for so long that I wondered what he was thinking in that adorable, but sometimes frustrating, little head of his. Did he understand it all? Did he remember? Petey squinted again, then squeezed his fist and jumped up and down to show joy, but he accidently crushed the bulb, and the light broke in jagged pieces in his palm.

"Get the tweezers!" Dad instructed.

I picked Petey up and hurried inside. As we entered the house, Petey grabbed the screen door with his bloody hand and held it open. Trying to pry his fingers from the door to administer first aid, I noticed that he was staring at the tree, smiling.

Twenty minutes later, with Petey's hand bandaged, Dad walked in with a tray of hot chocolate. Dad was trying hard to be Mom. Mom always made us hot chocolate when we put up the tree. Dad's chocolate wasn't smooth like Mom's had been. Dad's chocolate was lumpy and too heavy with chocolate powder that floated on top of the heated milk, like oil and water. It tasted good, though. Real good. Petey had some too, but he gulped so fast that he threw it right back up.

"It's the stimulation," Dad said and went back to the kitchen as I surveyed Petey's damage on the hardwood floors.

"He doesn't like change, even holiday change," I yelled. Dad returned with a large wad of paper towels and bent down to wipe the vomit off the polished floor. "He'll get used to Christmas and then get upset when we take it all down again."

"He doesn't want his routine disturbed. That's all." Dad wiped the last bit away. "I'll have to repolish the wood tomorrow," he said as he surveyed the floor.

"Choc . . ." I looked over at Petey, and so did Dad. "Choc!" Petey pointed to his empty cup.

"He said 'choc'!" I went over to Petey and bent down to eye level.

"You like the hot chocolate?"

Petey showed no emotion, but repeated his word. Then he sat down on the sofa, threw himself down, and fell asleep.

"Wish I could fall asleep like that," Dad said. I sat back down on the arm of his recliner.

"He said 'choc,'" I repeated.

"So?"

"It means, Dad, that Petey understood. He spoke."

"He's spoken before." Dad looked away and clicked on the TV with the remote.

"He hasn't spoken for two years, Dad." I turned down the volume on the television news. "It's important!"

"Yeah, well . . ." Dad paused in thought and sat down on the big recliner. He stared out the window at our newly planted pine in the front yard. I stared at our smaller, fake, green Christmas tree inside the living room. "Petey needs a school and an IEP. He also needs an aide, which reminds me. We have an appointment on Monday for the regional center." Dad sighed and looked down.

"Dad, Petey has potential," I said. Dad just put his arm around me. "There's something there in his little brain, working. I can see it." Dad wasn't convinced.

"Sure," he said and faked a small smile.

Even though it was January, it was still warm in California. It was weird. Palm trees and hot weather in January. It didn't seem natural somehow. At the Academy of the Fields, the pumpkins were gone and were nothing but dry, old vines. The grapes were gone too, but the land was being turned over for the next season. Some vegetables still grew in a small section, along with hardy flowers pushing up through the soil.

At this time of year in New York, there would be no leaves at all, snow might be on the ground, and New York pizza would be just a block away. I sighed and entered the Academy of the Fields ballet school with Petey in tow. He ran to his corner and sat as the music for the class began.

During the barre work, I felt a little dizzy. When I opened to à la seconde, I faltered. I caught myself and fell back in with the rhythm. At the center floor, I went into a simple glissade—ensemble combination—and felt dizzy again. I shook it off and continued. Later I stumbled on a fouetté count. I got a cramp in my leg, then lost my balance. I excused myself and sat down on the floor right next to Petey.

"I must be getting the flu," I said, holding my head with one hand and rubbing my calf muscle with the other. "And I got a cramp."

"It's a charley horse," Mrs. Cassidy said and helped me to rub it. "You should probably go home." Mrs. Cassidy said and helped me up.

"I'll be okay," I protested, but Mrs. Cassidy insisted.

"Home!" She smiled. "And feel better."

⸲℃⸲

Back home, I still felt dizzy. Dad said that I wasn't eating enough, so I gave in and ate a hamburger that he grilled in the backyard. In January! He was barbecuing in January! Maybe that's what was bothering me—this upside-down world of California. The whole environment made you dizzy, but the burger tasted good.

Upstairs in my bedroom, I felt better. Maybe I did need more food. I sat on the bed and opened my laptop. I wanted to see if Miss Irina had answered. The list of emails was the usual huge pile. Delete, delete, delete, no, undelete, delete the spam to get to the good stuff.

Nothing.

"Come on in, Petey," I said, and he climbed onto the bed and threw himself down on the pillow and fell into a deep sleep. I covered him up and kissed him on the head. I leaned back over to send an instant message to Liz, but I felt dizzy again.

"Maybe I am getting the flu," I spoke aloud. Worried, I closed my laptop. I picked Petey up and carried him to his bed, then returned to my own room.

As I got into bed myself, thoughts of Miss Irina drifted through my mind. I felt a deepening sadness in my heart, but I wanted to stay optimistic, so I tried to remember how it used to be instead. I remembered Miss Irina in class, counting and clapping her hands to the rhythm of the music and making mistakes with her English, which made her even more special. The whole scene inside my head made me smile, despite my sad heart.

I thought about Liz too, and whether I should even bother to email her when she didn't seem to care about me anymore, so I tried to assuage my hurt feelings with good memories of her too. I thought of us going together to her dorm room at Manhattan Dance almost every day. Liz had two roommates but wasn't friends with either of them; they were twin sisters who kept to themselves. I thought of the dorm where Liz didn't have parents to tell her what to do, only a dorm housemother, a lady named Mrs. Burkov. My heart lingered a moment on the thoughts of the Manhattan Dance dorm. I could have stayed there in New York if only Dad had the money . . . but I quickly quashed the thought. Dad hadn't had a choice, and he'd been so good to me since we arrived in California. Determined to think positively, I turned out my own lamp and went to sleep.

The next day, I felt worlds better and wondered why I'd made such a big deal about the lack of emails from Ms. Irina and Liz. It hurt, but I'd survive. I finished my makeup in the bedroom mirror and flew out to the bus. As I rode along, I'd thought about my article for the *Seneca 'Zine*, which I joined almost a month ago. I'd been writing as backup for the regular columnists, and Dad was pleased that I was more "well rounded" at high school. I wrote my article on better food in the cafeteria, and it was meant to change the policy at school. I thought it was a good piece, but I worried about what the editor might think.

After school I had a conflict, though. I had a *Seneca 'Zine* meeting, but Petey also had an appointment with the regional center that would decide on his treatment and care. As the bus rambled over the lumpy, country dirt road, I decided to hand in my article and feign sickness to get out of the journalism meeting. I had to go to the regional center. It was important for Petey.

⁂

The *Seneca 'Zine* meeting was in the science lab because the conference room in the library was being renovated. The editor, the vested, ginger-haired guy from my home-room, was deep in a pile of papers, obviously editing, and he looked annoyed that I disturbed him.

"I came to drop off my article for the *'Zine*." I waited for an answer.

"You're twenty minutes early," he said.

"I thought being early was a good thing, Ralph."

"Rafe." He looked even more annoyed now, and he took his glasses off. "The English pronunciation is 'Rafe' with a long 'a.' Raaaafe," he said for emphasis. "Get it straight."

"Oh." I backed off a little. "Raaaaafe" was a little rude, but he was handsome in an overly mature, corporate sort of way. Several girls entered.

"You new?" they asked. I shook my head.

"I was just talking to Ralph, I mean Rafe, about my article on the cafeteria food." Rafe shot a look at me.

"Isn't he just like Ralph Rackstraw in *H.M.S. Pinafore*?"

108

One girl giggled. Another girl took me by the hand and led me to their group.

"The drama club did the musical *H.M.S. Pinafore* last year, and ever since all the girls have been mad for Rafe."

I didn't know anything about *H.M.S. Pinafore* but Rafe sure fit his part as rude editor: His navy sweater vest and black slacks—not jeans, but slacks—his short, slightly curly, well-groomed hair, and his serious, journalistic attitude. He was the Editor of the Year, at least according to Seneca High's "District High School Award for Journalism," which sat at the school's entryway in the locked glass cabinet that contained football jerseys, Decathlon trophies, and a basketball from 1985.

Rafe also wore a blazer over his sweater vest—a blazer—just like I did on my first day. He was a spiritual, blazer-wearing soul mate, so rude or not, I couldn't be mad at him. Besides, he was devastatingly handsome behind his designer eyeglasses. The only thing Rafe was missing was a bow tie, which would have made him a little more geeky, but we had an award-winning *'Zine*, and he had a reputation to live up to.

"Where's your article?" Rafe sat in his editor's chair, actually the teacher's chair. I slapped my article on the science lab sink in front of him. "'Unhealthy Choices, Bad Scholarship.'" Rafe picked up the article from me. "Good title for the cafeteria problem," he said.

"I gotta g—" I hardly got the words out before he roped me in.

"Liked your review on the school's pop show," he said without looking up from my article. He had this amazing ability to read and talk at the same time, as if he were a cable news journalist or something. "Maybe I'll give you a column to write on 'The Arts.'" Rafe finally looked up and eyed me. His face then went crimson and his editorial attitude dissolved as he put his head down. "You're a ballet dancer, aren't you?" He looked up quickly, then averted his eyes again. I nodded. "Okay, you're our art critic now."

"That's great!" I smiled.

"And we need a small story for the inside back page, above the credits," he said without once looking up. "Review something good," he said and kept on reading. "Amanda and Tony . . . where are your articles on the failing algebra rates?" Rafe had no problem looking at the other two writers. I thought at first that Rafe was stuck up, but now I wondered if he was just shy. I took advantage of his inattention, though, and left. I might still make the school bus and hoped that Dad wouldn't leave for the regional center without me.

✿

"Petey!" I yelled. "Get off the chair!" I ran to Petey as I entered the house. He was sitting on top of Dad's recliner. Petey had already climbed the summit and was teetering at the top, unbalancing the chair. It tipped over before I could catch him.

Luckily, Petey was so small that when the chair flipped, he landed in the gap underneath. The weight of the chair didn't seriously injure him. But he bumped his head. Dad ran down the steps into the rec room.

"What happened?"

"Petey's all right, just a little scared, and there'll probably be a bruise." I sighed.

"A bruise'll look bad to the regional center. We'll never get an aide for him now." Dad stressed and hyperventilated. "It's okay, Dad. They understand that special-needs children sometimes get into scrapes." I tried to reassure myself as I looked back down at Petey, who had a big, red mark starting on his forehead. He hadn't cried out loud. He just whimpered after the chair hit him, and he let me comfort him for a moment. Then he turned away and ran upstairs.

❧

The nearest regional center to Apple Glen was fifty miles away on the other side of Napa Valley. With the hard-to-get appointment, we bundled Petey in the car and headed to the center with all of his papers—a list of his doctors in New York, his schools, his previous assessments—many, many previous assessments. We drove fifty miles, mostly in silence since Petey didn't talk—except saying "choc" at Christmastime—and Dad was lost in his own thoughts.

Dad actually looked like he enjoyed the scenery, though, gazing out the window now and then as Petey slept. Since Dad was driving, I gazed out the window too as we passed many houses, shopping centers, parks, old orchards, more vineyards, and farmland. I noticed a wood that looked kind of like maples, but were actually something else. I frowned as I missed the maple trees back east.

"Look, here it is." Dad turned into the parking lot of a small, shabby office building. We sat looking up at it in silence.

"Is this it?" I asked, but the answer was obvious. "Gosh, the center back in New York was five stories high."

"Says Regional Center," Dad stated. He looked around the area a bit nervously; he didn't want to go into the building right away, and checked his watch. "We got here a little early after all. Why don't we eat something." It was avoidance, I could tell. There was a family-style restaurant across the street.

"Over there!" I pointed, and woke Petey up.

"He should be well rested now for the visit," I said as I released him from the seat belt.

"And with food in his stomach, he should be more manageable . . . unless it disagrees with him." Dad gave me a wary look, and we walked across the street to the restaurant.

At the restaurant, Petey played with his pancakes and got syrup all over his hands. I wiped them off and tried to eat my chicken Caesar salad, but it was useless. Petey got his hands all sticky again playing with the food, and I didn't get to finish my own lunch.

"Let's go," I said, anxious to get it over with.

The office of the center was busy with parents and children with all variations of special needs. There was a long line for the counter, so I left Petey with Dad and then returned with a yellow slip.

"We have an appointment, so we go to the blue corner." I pointed and led them to the blue area, where we were stuck with another line. Again, Dad waited with Petey while I filled out the forms. I felt like Petey's second mother sometimes. Waving to Petey, I saw that he ignored me but touched some toys near the chairs. As I reached the front of the line, I gave the forms to the woman at the desk, then sat with Dad and Petey, and waited . . . and waited . . .

"Mr. Sutton . . ." I looked over as I heard Dad's name being called. I saw a middle-aged black woman holding a folder. "Nice to meet you. I'm Jackie Martins and you must be Peter." Petey responded with a grunt.

"This is my daughter, Kendra. She came with us today because she's good with Petey."

"Nice to meet you," I responded earnestly. Ms. Martins pointed to a nearby office and we all followed her.

Inside, Jackie Martins threw her folder down onto the desk and sat down with a thud.

"These tired old bones are getting too old for all this," she said as she indicated her office, which was in disarray. File folders sat outside of the drawers, on tables, and among labeled boxes that were probably case files for other children. I looked more closely at this woman who was going to help my brother. If she was this messy, how would she help Petey?

"Now . . . you need resources for . . ." Jackie perused Petey's folder. "Apple Glen, or nearby Marbury—"

"Apple Glen, if possible," I interrupted. Jackie Martins looked up from her folder.

"Not much for Apple Glen, I'm afraid. There are more resources in Marbury. That's about . . ."

"Five miles away." Dad shook his head. "I need something close because I work and my daughter's in school—"

"I'm afraid the only option is a somewhat mediocre school on the outskirts of Napa Valley, but . . ." Jackie hesitated. "We can still try to get him into the better school."

"What's the name of that one?" I asked.

"York," Jackie replied.

"Is it a center or a school?" I asked.

"It's a school, and a very nice one too. Only trouble is they take children on the higher end of the autistic spectrum." I immediately put my head down. "But we can call them, see what they say." Jackie smiled a reassuring smile. "Maybe we can pull some strings." I hugged Petey, who promptly pushed me away, not wanting to be touched again, but my heart jumped anyway with hope.

The next morning, I pulled the brush through my long brown hair, which had just been shampooed, conditioned, blown dry, moussed, and gel-shined to perfection. The sound of the rain pelting the windowpanes, though, would not go too well with freshly moussed hair. I thought it never rained in "sunny California." I stared out at the pelting rain again. The smell of damp air entered the room through a crack in the window and made the morning seem gloomier, which brought me back to Petey's situation.

Jackie Martins's ability to pull strings wasn't what she had promised. Petey had to go to the mediocre school after all. Williamson Special Needs School—I even hated the name of it. Did they have to point out that kids like Petey were different? Couldn't they have just called it Williamson? At least it was only a day school and he'd be home before I got home from my school. He could still go to ballet class with me. I heard the rain again and sighed.

I searched for Petey to say good-bye for the day, but I couldn't find him. He was hiding. I realized where he was—in the closet of his room, sitting, flapping, lost in his own world. It was an ordeal getting him ready in the morning: putting him in the red shirt and green pants and combing his hair when he didn't want to be touched. He often threw tantrums. The tribulations of combing his hair would start a war that would go on for half an hour. We always had to leave time in our schedule to get through the hair-combing nightmare.

Petey didn't want to go to the new school. What if they were abusive to him there? How would I know? I was at my own school all day, but it was the only option we had. Maybe my imagination ran away with me. Petey didn't like change. Transitions were extremely difficult. He needed routine, and his routine had been upset by the move to California, the new house, the new school . . .

"Peteeeeeyyy!" My voice echoed down the hall as I walked to his room. I opened the closet door to find him in the corner sitting in the dark, just like I thought. "Come on, Petey. Time to go." Petey pulled back as I took his hand. I felt like a traitor. He looked at me with fear in his eyes, and I just couldn't make him come out to go to a school he didn't like. Dad entered the room and pulled him out of the closet, and Petey clung to a plastic hanger for comfort. I took the hanger out of his hands. "Ready?"

"Wait! His hair!" Dad warned.

"Forget it!" I said. "We'll be late." I smoothed his hair back with my fingers, then ruffled it up like a punk rocker. "There! Now he looks trendy."

"Yeah, if red and green is the new black." Dad smiled.

❧

We pulled up to Williamson as the rain stopped, and Petey stared at the building from the backseat.

"I'll take him in," I volunteered. "I haven't seen the place yet."

"It's all right inside. Not great, but okay, I guess." Dad

sighed, knowing that nothing but the best was good enough for Petey, but unfortunately, the best was not available.

I unbuckled Petey from the seat and pulled him along, but he dragged his feet, making it twice as hard to get him to the entrance of the school.

"Uh," Petey grunted.

"It's okay, Petey. It's like kindergarten." I lifted him and carried him inside. "Lots of kids feel that way. You'll get used to it."

As we entered the school, I saw kids in lines waiting to go to their classrooms, with teacher's aides beside them. Parents dropped their children off and left for work while breakfast trays with oatmeal were lined up on a table in the hall by the staff.

"I'll take him." The voice surprised me. It was Petey's aide. She smiled a little, and I released him to her.

"I'll see you later, Petey." I kissed him on the head and left. Turning back I saw sadness in Petey's eyes. It looked like he wanted to cry, but he never cried real tears. He just stared longingly, and I felt my heart tear in two.

"I think we need to do a surprise visit." Back in the car, I looked Dad straight in the eyes. "Call in sick for me, Dad."

"You can't miss school."

"I already missed the bus. Besides, this is important," I insisted. "We need to see what it's like when we're not supposed to be there." Dad was reluctant, but he knew I was right.

"Okay," he said, and we drove back home in silence.

❧

At one o'clock, Dad and I drove back to Williamson School. As we headed inside the building that was quiet and orderly in the morning, I heard yelling from kids in different rooms. Two teachers ran down the hall after a little boy, who disappeared around the corner, and in the hall I noticed toilet paper on the floor. As we walked down the hallway, nobody even asked us who we were or what we were doing there. Nevertheless, we headed toward Petey's room and looked in the window on the classroom door.

There was only one teacher in the room, and she was on her cell phone gabbing. Kids ran around willy-nilly, some climbing on the teacher's desk; others threw blocks at each another. Kids sat like zombies on chairs, too, as extremely loud music blared from a boom box.

"I can't believe this!" Dad opened the door and shouted. "Hey, you!" The aide looked up, embarrassed, and dropped her phone.

I turned the music off and stepped on a food tray filled with old oatmeal from breakfast, and it made me sick. A little girl had been eating the now congealed mess and had it all over her face. As I stared at the unsupervised scene, I noticed that Petey was nowhere to be seen.

"Where's Petey?" Looking around the room, I stepped over kid after kid, searching for my brother.

"Uh." Petey's grunt came from below.

"Here he is," Dad said, and I saw him under a table, rocking in a fetal position. Another boy sat next to him, eating Petey's crackers. Dad grabbed Petey, then I looked around at the other special needs kids. They looked so lost. There was definitely no nurturing going on at this place.

"Where's the staff?" Dad shouted again.

"*No hablo Inglés.*"

"There's supposed to be three aides in the room," I added.

"*Está enferma* . . . sick," the aide answered.

"This is unacceptable," Dad stated, lowering his voice again.

"*Sí*, alone . . . me solo."

"I'm going to talk to the front desk." Dad gave Petey to me and left for a moment. The aide looked worried.

"*Trabajo mucho!*" she cried.

"You need help," I said sympathetically.

"Sí." She smiled, understanding that.

I stared at the kids in the room and got an idea. Turning the boom box back on, I found a gentler, calming tune. Immediately, the kids looked at me and began to settle down, but Petey was still upset. I wanted to bolt immediately with him, but somehow I couldn't leave these terribly sad little kids.

Taking Petey's hands, I started to dance with him slowly like we did at home. It worked. Petey's squint came back. The other kids started to move around, some feeling the music and others ignoring it. I took another girl's hand and danced with her a little, and she smiled, then shrunk back. The aide did the same and seemed surprised that the kids responded. A little boy imitated Petey and did a little dance of his own. Half of the room now swayed to the music, and the ones who felt the music and moved made a real connection.

I noticed how they reacted positively to the soft music. Out of this horrible little day-care center, dance made all the difference in their afternoon. Somehow it made me smile too. Here I was, dancing not in a ballet class or onstage, but with a group of autistic children, and it made me feel really great.

"The school website said we can visit at any time, so we visited," Dad said as he returned with the head of the school.

"I'm so sorry that this happened. I assure you that it will never happen again."

"I hope not," Dad stated. He was still steamed.

"Is there anything we can do to make this better?" I could tell that the administrator felt uncomfortable as she hyperventilated a little.

"Yeah," I said. "Let me volunteer here." The administrator looked at me oddly. "I could come in two days a week and help exercise the kids."

"But your ballet . . . and the *'Zine . . .*" Dad moved toward me.

"Ballet isn't until four thirty, and I can email the *'Zine . . .* I could be here at three o'clock after school, two days a week." I turned toward the administrator. "I'm a dancer. I can do movement with them for an hour. Work with them through music." The administrator was on the spot but seemed to know it might be a way out of the indelicate predicament.

"Well, you'd have to get clearance, but . . . it might work. Give them something to look forward to." The administrator shook her head. I turned the boom box back on and the kids swayed to the music again, and some of them actually smiled. Petey grunted and squinted.

"It's okay, boy." Dad hugged Petey and smiled at me. "I think it's going to be okay now."

Chapter Ten

Several days later, I went back to Williamson School. The administrator gave me clearance to volunteer, and I planned a fun workout for the kids from three to four o'clock. I brought some CDs with me and figured I'd start slowly to gain their confidence. Then I'd build a rapport, and they would express themselves more and have fun with dance.

The room had been cleaned up a lot. There were several aides now in the room, but the kids were the same—stoic zombies or wildly out of control. Petey sat on a chair, eating his crackers until a kid grabbed them from his hand. There was no reaction in my brother's face.

"Fight back," I whispered but knew he was unable to do so. Petey then recognized me and ran to cling to my leg. The other aides sat down when they saw me and clapped for the kids' attention.

"Miss Sutton is here. Sit down," they shouted to the kids.

"I'm Kendra," I said. The two aides didn't introduce themselves, but the aide from the other day walked up to me.

"Bea," she said. "Beatriz."

"Hi, Bea," I said. "How are you today?"

"She's from Panama. She can't speak much English," an aide interrupted. The second aide spoke. "It doesn't matter. Most of the kids don't speak much anyway."

I couldn't believe that they underestimated the kids like that. I put a CD into the boom box, spread a large, colored, rubber mat on the floor, and Bea helped me round up the children.

"Okay, let's get started. Are you ready to dance?" I looked at the kids and smiled.

I sat down on the floor and started to stretch. Some of the kids imitated me.

"Good!" I said. After stretching, I stood up and stretched up into the air in time to the music. "Reach for the sky!" Some kids followed me, but some of them just sat back and watched, oblivious. Petey stretched with me and squinted a lot.

"We're gonna move." I danced over to the boom box and changed the tempo of the music and waved my arms in the air. The kids followed me in a march around a circle on the mat, and then we wiggled and laughed and wiggled again.

"Here we go!" Only a few of the kids responded fully. Some of them moved their hands or flapped, and others did nothing at all. I then tried dancing with each of them.

"Turn around, and up and down." Some moved awkwardly and others lost interest. A few of them had problems with motor skills and couldn't quite do the movements, but the important part was they tried. One boy lay down in the middle and fell asleep, and Bea had to move him.

The clock quickly moved to four o'clock, so I waved good-bye to the kids. Some cried when I left and others didn't care at all. As I drove to the Cassidy's' with Petey, I wondered whether I had made a difference with any of them. I could tell that I'd reached some of them, but I wanted to reach them all.

⟨⟩

As soon as we entered the Academy of the Fields, Petey ran to his corner, grabbed a pink tutu, and watched us at the barre. His mood improved almost immediately. Again, it was something about the music, the movement . . . I knew I was on to something.

As I did my own barre work, I turned to stretch my leg upon the barre. I felt almost like prima Alyssa Trent as I moved. With my leg still on the wood, I bent my head down in port de bras to touch my ankle and lost my balance. I grabbed the barre to catch my fall.

Becca caught me. "Are you okay?" I felt dazed for a moment and got another cramp in my leg muscle.

"Owwww."

Mrs. Cassidy ran over. "The cramp again?"

I nodded, too full of pain to respond.

"Relax the muscle. The charley horse will go away. Relax." Mrs. Cassidy rubbed my muscle and I did my best to relax. The room spun once or twice as I tried to concentrate on my muscle.

"It's going away," I said, rubbing my calf, but the dizziness was still with me.

"Can you stand up?"

I nodded and tried to get up, but then everything turned black and I went limp.

"Kendra?" I heard my name from afar, as if I were in a tunnel. "Kendra?" It was clearer now. The blackness began to fade away and I saw Mrs. Cassidy's face close to mine.

"Kendra?"

I opened my eyes more.

"You fainted." I realized that she was right. My leg muscle didn't contract violently like it had just moments before, but my dizziness continued. I tried to get up but couldn't.

"I have to sit down," I said.

"Get her some water," Mrs. Cassidy ordered. "She may be dehydrated." Becca got a water bottle from the school's vending machine and brought it over to me. I drank it, thirsty.

"You're probably just dehydrated, Kendra. It affects the muscles."

"It could be diabetes. Thirst is a big symptom," Becca said.

Mrs. Cassidy threw a warning look at her, then asked, "Do you have any dizziness?"

"Yes, dizziness too."

"I'm going to call your dad to make an appointment for the doctor," Mrs. Cassidy said. "You've been doing too much since you came to California. Petey is a big responsibility, and you've been working too hard for the audition." I didn't answer. I drank more of the water. I think I swallowed more than half the bottle.

"You're right. I was just dehydrated." I stood up straighter. "I'll have to watch it, is all."

"You fainted. That's not good." Mrs. Cassidy looked concerned. "You are going to see a doctor before you come back to class this week." My face went into protest mode, but she insisted. I gathered Petey up and got ready to go out to the car.

"Are you sure you can drive?" Becca asked, concerned.

"She's not driving." Mrs. Cassidy turned. "Troy, drive them home and, Becca, follow them with the car."

"I'm fine, really—"

"Troy's driving. There are two of you to worry about." Mrs. Cassidy smiled at Petey, who squinted back.

Troy got behind the wheel and Becca followed us in her mother's blue car. As we took off down Chapel Street, I waved to Mrs. Cassidy and looked back over at Troy.

I have really good friends, I thought, my heart warming over. I waved back to Becca in the car behind us. "Thanks."

"I'll never pass up a chance to drive a pretty girl home." Troy smiled. "Gotta live up to my reputation." I was about to become annoyed again with his bravado, but I saw something in Troy's smile that held a tinge of sincerity. He looked at me halfway through the red light with a goofy look on his face.

"Watch the road," I warned, but I began to think that maybe he really meant it. Did he really mean it? Did he think I was pretty? Not knowing what to do, I just punched him lightly in the arm and laughed. After all, I kind of liked Rafe, and Troy was just a friend, wasn't he?

At the doctor's office the next day, I sat on the bed in the examination room in a white paper dress. Actually, it was two white dresses, with one turned backward to cover everything, you know. I had my underwear and bra but still felt shy. I was really modest and hated going to the doctor's for that reason. Everything crinkled—the paper dress, the paper on the bed.

I thumbed through a magazine so I wouldn't be nervous, but it wasn't working. The smell of alcohol and medicines permeated the room, assuring me that I was in a medical place. The room was so cold too, as if they had the air conditioner on high. What if sick people got pneumonia? I shivered in the paper dress, which crinkled again.

The nurse took my blood pressure and temperature, and asked me all kinds of questions. The doctor came in briefly to check my heartbeat and had the nurse come back to do a blood test. I had to pee in a little plastic cup too. It was so undignified.

The sound of footsteps outside my room made me look up. The handle on the door turned, then stopped. I heard the doctor's voice again, talking to one of the nurses as he held the door partially open. Then he entered, and a nurse followed behind him and smiled at me.

"The blood test will be back in a few days. I think you'll be all right," he said.

"Thank goodness," I replied.

"If the dizziness and muscle cramps reoccur, have your dad schedule another visit. But I'm pretty sure that it's just stress from the move, and, like your teacher said, you do have a lot of responsibility with Petey. I'll talk to your father about that."

"No, it's okay. I take care of Petey because I love him."

"You're also working at your brother's school. It's too much."

"I'm an overachiever?" I joked.

"Well, maybe it's just overworked muscles, then," the doctor said.

"That's what my father says." I looked down at my leg muscles and rubbed my left calf.

"Take it easy. Don't be so hard on yourself." The doctor smiled and walked out of the room.

❦

With the doctor visit out of the way, life went back to normal. Every week, Becca, Troy, and I would wind up at a movie on Saturday night with dinner at a Mexican restaurant afterwards. As much as I missed New York pizza, I fell in love with Mexican food. There were a few Mexican chain restaurants in the city, but I'd never had time to try one before. Here in California, Mexican food was plentiful and home cooked, and we ate it often.

"The movie really freaked me out," Becca said. "I don't want to see anything scary like that ever again."

"Me either!" I said between bites of beans and rice. I couldn't stuff it in my mouth fast enough. I felt better, and even though the food was highly fattening and not good for keeping my body in elite form, it was my once-a-week feast. and I wolfed it down.

"Next time, let's go to a comedy," I said as I eyed the Mexican restaurant's décor.

"Comedy, drama, historical, scary, blockbuster, animated. We have to do them in order. You know the rules."

Becca and I laughed at Troy's insistence.

"Can't we skip 'scary' and go for two comedies instead?" Becca's eyes widened.

"Depends on what's playing," I answered. It's not a megacity multiplex, you know!" I ate the last two forkfuls of my enchilada and scraped up the last of the refried beans with cheese.

"Whoa there, girl!" Troy laughed. "This girl hasn't eaten in weeks!"

"Get her another plate!" Becca said.

"No." I laughed and waved my fork in the air. "One dinner is definitely enough!" Becca was fun. She made me laugh a lot, especially when she thought she had the "disease of the week."

Just then I thought about Liz, my BFF back in New York. Liz used to make me laugh a lot too with her imitations and silly remarks. But I hadn't heard from Liz lately. She'd started hanging around that awful Sara Harrington, who got my snowflake part. I watched it all unfold on my Facebook page. Liz had emailed me finally, but then her emails got less and less frequent . . . until they stopped. I stared at my email every night, just like I did for Miss Irina, hoping that Liz would write, but I guess she wasn't a friend anymore. How could people just stop being friends?

I looked over at Becca finishing up her dinner. Would Becca ever stop being friends with me if I moved back to New York? How could you tell which friends were true?

"I have to go to the restroom," Becca said, holding her stomach.

"Me too," I added.

"And leave me alone at the table with no girls," Troy joked. "What about my reputation?"

"Seems to me it's a little inflated," Becca said and groaned, holding her stomach. "Besides, one night without girls won't kill you."

"You have no idea," Troy said and held his heart.

"Hey! Kendra's a girl." Becca laughed.

"But Troy and I are just friends, and we'll keep it that

way." I smiled at Troy and meant it as a joke, but I think I might have hurt Troy's feelings. He stopped smiling and looked down. I wondered if I had said the wrong thing, but as I stood up, my right leg gave way, and Becca reached out and caught me.

"Are you all right?" she asked.

I couldn't get a grip on my footing and held my leg. I knelt down on the floor to bolster myself, then tried to rise again. I grasped the table, accidentally pushing off some of the silverware, which made a loud clang. I felt totally embarrassed.

"I . . . I can't get up," I said and looked up at the Mexican artwork on the colored walls of the restaurant, which made me dizzy. The smell of the beans and rice suddenly made me feel sick too.

"Drugs!" A businessman said as he walked by. Disgusted. Becca turned and yelled, "Mind your own business, jerk!" Troy now got up and lifted me back into my chair.

"What's wrong?" He really looked concerned, and it touched my heart momentarily, but my leg went into spasms and then went numb too.

"My leg fell asleep." I covered well as the feeling came back into my calf muscle.

"What's going on with you, Kendra?" Troy asked, concerned. "You're not drinking any of that Academy of the Fields vino."

"No, she's not!" Becca interrupted and threw a look now at Troy. "Are you okay?"

I didn't know what else to say.

"I don't know."

Chapter Eleven

I want to explore all possibilities to rule out or diagnose the symptoms and cause, so I am referring you to a neurologist—"

"A neurologist?" My dad and I spoke together. The doctor looked a little uncomfortable and squirmed in his chair. "Why a neurologist?" my dad asked.

"There could be some type of damage to a nerve, in the brain or spinal cord. It's just regular procedure to check it out." The doctor opened the file on his desk. "I'm also ordering an MRI for Kendra."

"An MRI?" My fear of doctor's offices came into full bloom. "What's an MRI?"

"It's an imaging machine. It'll take pictures inside your brain."

"It's like a metal tube, isn't it?" Dad looked worried, which didn't make me feel any better.

"You'll be in there for a few minutes."

"How many minutes?" My heart started palpitating.

"Twenty."

I suddenly felt like I was going to pass out again.

"No, no . . ."

"Not to worry. I hear you're pretty smart. Maybe your brain'll look like Einstein's." The doctor tried his best to make me laugh. I didn't feel like laughing.

"Do you think it's anything serious?" My dad looked shaken up.

"We just have to check it all out." He finished writing on a slip of paper and handed it to Dad. "Just procedure."

Maybe it was just procedure to Dr. Meyer, but it was major to me. Dad, Petey, and I walked out of Dr. Meyer's office and headed for our car in the medical building's parking lot. It was raining so we had to run for it. Once inside, I buckled up a wet, cranky Petey. Then I got in front and put my feet up on the dashboard and hugged my ankles. Dad didn't even say anything about putting my feet up.

"I'm sure it'll be nothing, hon." Dad smiled confidently as he started up the car.

"Maybe not for you." My voice shook as Petey kicked the back of my seat.

"I'll be there with you the whole time."

"Thanks, Dad." I could hardly get the words out. Dad smiled again and pinched my cheek lightly. As we drove, the rain pelted the car windows so hard that it seemed like the sky broke. I was lost in a sea of self-pity, but Dad looked straight ahead through all the driving rain. I knew he was worried, though, because he avoided looking at me the rest of the way home.

The neurologist's office was bigger than Dr. Meyer's, and it was in a big hospital. We waited with Petey in the beautiful waiting room with mood music piped in through the walls. There were a lot of good beauty magazines to read here. I was nervous so I scooped up about ten of them to bring into the inner office. Then I felt selfish and put three of them back on the waiting room table.

"That's us," Dad said and waved for me to go in.

"You can come too, Mr. Sutton. It's just vision and motor skills testing."

We all walked into the inner office and the nurse sat me down at a table where I saw colored blocks. Petey looked around at the brightly colored walls too. A woman came into the room, looking very doctor-y, and said hello.

"How are you this morning?"

"Perfect!" I blurted.

"Don't be scared. We're just testing today." The nurse took out a deck of cards, but they weren't regular playing cards. They had figures on them. She flipped a card.

"Kendra, I want you to draw the figure on this card." It seemed babyish, but I did it. She flipped another card and then another and another. I was never good at drawing, but I did all right. My pen faltered once or twice, but that's because I was nervous. The woman then checked my vision, reflexes, and motor skills, having me catch balls and open and close my hands and stuff like that. The specialist visit wasn't so bad, but it seemed kind of stupid.

Later at home, I sat at the dinner table, nibbling my chicken potpie. Petey was tired from the day and put his head on the table, the contents of potpie all over his face.

"I wonder if they can really tell anything with those stupid tests," I said.

"Ow!" Dad accidentally burned himself with the steam from his own dinner. "I'll have to contact the HMO."

"For the MRI?"

"No. For this burn!" He looked serious for a minute, then broke out laughing.

"Stop it, Dad! I still have the MRI this week and I'm scared."

"You know I'll be with you."

I didn't answer. I just picked all of the peas out of my potpie with my fork and placed them on the plate below. My plate now looked just as bad as Petey's. "Eat, honey." I couldn't. I put my fork down with a clang.

"What if I can't dance?"

"Dancing's in your blood," Dad said.

"No. I mean it. What if I don't dance again? What if that happens?" My body trembled. Dad looked more serious now, and he stared off into space.

"He said if you have . . ."

"What? Say it, Dad!" I wanted to cry. "No, don't say it." If it wasn't said, it wouldn't happen.

"Remember the time you had to go to the dentist to get your teeth pulled?"

I nodded my head yes. "I was eleven."

"The dentist had to put you to sleep to have all four back teeth taken out to make room for your molars."

"And my braces . . ."

"Remember how scared you were?"

I did remember. "And you told me that it was going to be all right. And it was."

"You woke up in the dentist's chair, and you asked me—"

"When are they going to pull my teeth?" I laughed a little, because I'd forgotten all about it.

"No," Dad corrected me. "You said, 'Whan rrrr the goona pull my ttth?'" I laughed a little more. "You had a mouthful of cotton. You didn't even know they had already done it." Dad laughed, and so did I. I felt almost slaphappy now and didn't know whether to laugh or cry.

Then Dad surprised me. He got up from the table, walked over, and bent down to eye level with me. "You forgot all about the dentist within one week," Dad said. "The same thing's gonna happen this time with the MRI, Kendra." Dad grabbed me tighter. "You'll be okay."

Tears rolled down my cheeks, and I felt like a little girl again, about to go to the dentist. I knew my dad would try to make it all right somehow. But this wasn't a cosmetic procedure. It was more serious. Could I die?

I hugged Dad as tightly as he hugged me and cried right into his shoulder, soaking his red flannel shirt right through.

❧

Monday morning at six I stood in front of the big, gray monster. I felt like a paper doll in my crinkly blue paper dress. As I stared at the machine that might eat me alive, I trembled. Dad stood beside me, but I couldn't stop shaking.

"It looks different than the one I saw on the Internet." I stared at the machine.

"I told them you were scared, so they are putting you into an open MRI."

"Okay."

"I'll be right there, behind the glass." Dad pointed, and I looked over to where a technician behind glass stood adjusting some equipment. The tech waved and came over. He had a needle in his hand.

"Hi, my name's Alberto." He shook my hand and Dad's too. "Now you'll lie down on this panel, and we'll slide you in. It won't hurt a bit."

"That might," I said, indicating the needle.

"It's a contrast dye, gadolinium. Now hold steady. It won't hurt either."

"Huh." I couldn't speak. I froze. He was right. The needle didn't hurt much as the dye went into my body.

"It will highlight any tissues around your spine and brain, just to be sure that we can see everything." Alberto put the needle on a table and readjusted the panel that slid out of the machine. "Now lie down."

"Okay." I climbed up, and lay down on the MRI panel bed. Alberto placed my head on a headrest. Then he placed what looked like a wire around me. I felt strapped in, as if I were on a weird ride at some strange theme park.

"Ready?" Alberto smiled reassuringly.

I looked over at Dad, who now stood behind the glass. He winked, then pointed to his teeth and pretended that a dentist was yanking them out. It made me laugh out of nervousness or just plain fear.

"That's the spirit," said Alberto, but I stopped laughing as the moment of entry came closer.

"Will it hurt?"

"Not at all. I promise. Are you ready?" Alberto repeated his question, and I nodded. Alberto then started the machine, which pushed me slowly into the abyss of the blue-and-gray tubular world that swallowed me up like the monster I feared it to be.

I panicked. I felt claustrophobic inside. "Stop!" I said. Even though I could see out the sides of the machine, I banged on the walls and heard my voice echo.

"Let me out!" I breathed rapidly. Alberto slid me out again.

"Don't bang on the equipment. It's expensive!"

"I'm sorry." I sat up apprehensively, breathing fast from fear. Alberto handed me a device that looked like a TV remote.

"Hold this," he said. "If you feel panicky, just press the button, and we'll slide you out. Don't bang."

"What if I can't do it?" I was really scared. Would they give me a sedative like Dad said? I didn't see any sedative in sight and gulped. "What if I panic and can't do it?"

"I'll talk to you. There's a speaker in there. You'll hear my voice."

"Okay."

"I'll explain everything that's happening as I do it." That made me calmer. Knowing what was happening helped a lot.

"How long will it take?"

"About thirty minutes."

"Thirty?"

Alberto grabbed hold of the little bed. "Ready?" I nodded my head, unsure, but there was little choice.

"Okay," I agreed, and he sent the bed back in slowly. When I was inside, like a hot dog in a bun, I almost panicked again. I wondered if I would turn into toast, but then remembered that I held the remote. I pressed the button.

"Already?" I heard the bemused voice of the technician who was behind a glass. He laughed. "It's only been a minute. You can't be scared yet!"

"Yes, I can," I answered.

"Breathe," the tech said. "Take two long, deep breaths." The two deep breaths did calm me down. "Remember that you have the controller. Try to stay calm, but if you really panic, you have the device. You can push it and we'll take you out."

Alberto waited for my answer. I looked back at him through the tunnel of the machine and examined his face as he stood behind the glass. He had large, friendly eyes, and he looked like someone's dad. Somehow his fatherly face reassured me.

"Okay," my voice quivered. My body was like Jell-O.

"Here we go," he said. I heard a large noise, like construction going on outside. Jackhammers. The thunder of pounding grew louder.

"The noise is the machine taking pictures." The tech's voice shouted through the remote. "Are you okay in there?"

"Yeah!" I shouted and the sound echoed back, hurting my ears.

"Try not to move or talk." I shook my head, but the tech couldn't see me. I then closed my eyes. I tried to think of dancing as a snowflake in *The Nutcracker* and realized just how far away from New York and *The Nutcracker* I really was at that very moment. Tears rolled down my face from my closed eyes, and I just wanted it all to be a dream, a very bad dream . . . that I never left New York . . . that I never had to be dizzy . . . that I never had to be in this MRI machine. My heart pounded as loud as the machine did.

When I opened my eyes, I was in a little room on a bed. There were white walls all around.

"Did I die?" I whispered out to the universe.

"You're in a recovery room." Dad's face came into focus. He looked down at me on the bed. "You fainted again." I looked around, grateful that I was out of that awful machine. Then a terrible thought hit me.

"I don't have to do it all over again?"

"No." Dad smiled. "You're done."

Alberto hovered over me now. Relief flooded through my system when I saw the technician's fatherly face come into view as well.

"As soon as you feel up to it, you can leave, Sleeping Beauty." I popped up from the bed and felt a little weak. Dad helped me up, though. He knew I wanted to get out of there.

❧

A few days later, Dad and I sat in the doctor's office again. Petey played with a train toy he brought from home, and I curled up on the chair in a fetal position and grabbed my ankles.

"What's the prognosis?" Dad came right to the point. The doctor opened my folder and perused it for a full minute. I was freaking out inside.

"The assessment indicates that Kendra"—he looked over at me—"may have the beginnings of multiple sclerosis."

"MS?" Dad was shocked and got up from his chair. He paced back and forth in the little room.

"It's damage to the nerve in the brain or the spinal cord. It's degenerative." I was puzzled.

"What does that mean?" I asked.

"It means that you could lose the ability to walk, or you could experience dizziness enough to interfere with your dancing."

"No!" I stood up, outraged. My entire life of lessons, costumes, and dreaming flashed before my eyes as I sputtered out the words, "I can't be sick!"

"I'm sorry, Kendra."

"No!" I yelled. Dad grabbed me and sat me back down.

"What'll happen?" Dad was beside himself. He looked at Petey, then me. I could tell he felt overwhelmed with two medical problems now in his life.

"It means that you may continue to feel dizzy, have cramps in your muscles. You may lose some fine motor skills."

"The skills I need for ballet?" I whispered.

"Exactly. You might lose control of one or more of your limbs."

"Oh my g—" I burst out wanting to cry, but the tears wouldn't come. His words stunned me.

"You could have all of these symptoms." He hesitated. "Or you could have none." He paused again. "That's the trouble with this disease. The symptoms mimic other diseases, and they can come and go. You have a problem with a nerve in your spinal cord, Kendra, which regulates fine motor skills."

"What causes it?" Dad was trying to be reasonable as I hyperventilated in my chair.

"It's the myelin sheath, which is unprotected . . ."

I put my head on the doctor's desk, blocking out his words. I closed my eyes in defeat.

All the fight I put into going back to New York was gone. I would end up in a wheelchair, never dance at Manhattan Dance, and die here of MS.

"The medicine can control the relapses . . ." Dr. Meyer's voice went in and out as I fell into nothingness. ". . . if she has any. We'll see . . ." Dr. Meyer stopped speaking. Dad put his arm around me, and Petey came over and touched my head as well.

"Uh," Petey grunted. I lifted my head, not wanting to alarm my brother. He pointed to a bird on a tree outside. "Uh," he grunted again.

"Kendra," Dr. Meyer spoke. "There are medications to control it. With medication and injections you might have a completely normal life."

"Or she could become disabled."

I stared at Dad in disbelief. "You're not helping!" My voice wavered as I sat down again in tears, and he grabbed my hand.

"Will the injections really help? Will she be able to have a career as a dancer?"

The doctor gave us his professional smile.

"There's a lot of research going on right now. I've looked up other cases similar to yours—athletes, painters . . . Many have been helped by the medicines, and they live quite normal lives."

"So, there's hope?" I looked at the doctor with a pleading face. The doctor nodded, and my heart leaped. "Will I be able to join the company?" The doctor didn't answer right away.

"It's a crapshoot," he said. "You could join the company and be just fine with medication, or you could join and go into a relapse onstage. We just don't know." I breathed out, like I had just been hit in the stomach by a boxer's KO punch.

⟨≈⟩

When we got home from the doctor's, I jumped out of Dad's car and right into mine. I couldn't get out of there fast enough. I drove away as quickly as I could but saw Dad in the side mirror, waving frantically for me to come back.

Turning onto the freeway, I got into a crowded lane and just drove and drove. I didn't care where. I then saw a sign that said, "San Francisco," and followed the line of cars.

Pushing the gas pedal, I vented my emotion into the drive. Changing lanes, I almost bumped into another car, and it scared me, so I slowed down a little.

I don't remember what I saw or how many miles I drove. I put in a CD and listened to the music, but it was ballet music. Most of my CDs were ballet music. There was no getting away from it, but the background noise made me feel a little normal again.

My thoughts swirled around my head like a tornado in a bottle, and even though I tried not to think about the doctor's office, I couldn't help it. My mind was in overdrive. I wanted to cry, but terror of the freeway caused me to grip the steering wheel, and I felt every muscle in my body tense.

A large truck roared as it drove by me in the next lane. The oversized vehicle went on and on like a dragon that never ended. It stressed me out until, finally, it passed, and a car playing loud salsa drowned out my ballet music and whizzed by too.

I continued to drive. My disease loomed much larger on my mind than being in an accident or the oversized Mac truck.

"How could I have MS?" I asked aloud. The ballet score on my player crescendoed at that moment, and a clash of cymbals highlighted the *Swan Lake* music by Tchaikovsky. It was dramatic music. Ballet always had dramatic music. If you didn't know it was made for ballet, you might think it was music for a horror movie, except when the music was sweet and carried you away.

"What if I can't dance? What if . . ." As I listened to the music, my breathing became rapid. I felt as if I was going to faint. I slammed the button on the CD player, and the disc popped out. Grabbing it in one hand, I opened the window and threw it out into the noisy air of the freeway. I needed to get rid of it. Get it out of my mind. But it didn't stop. The familiar music played in my mind over and over, making me think of the mess my life was in. The MRI, the company audition . . . My mind became a collage of everything that went wrong ever since we came to California. And what if I couldn't dance? That's all I could think of over and over again. My chest heaved with anxiety. It wasn't fair. I just wanted to die.

Driving for what seemed like days, I looked for the sign that led to San Francisco, but I couldn't find it. I noticed that the landscape had changed. There were no more vineyards or farmland; there was nothing but scrub brush and dirt, and in the distance, an expanse of ocean scenery. I realized I was on the coast somewhere.

I think I got lost.

There were big mountains and tourist spots ahead. I saw families camping out nearby, people swimming, and even surfers catching a wave out in the water. I'd never seen surfers in person before. I had to see them up close.

The blue of the water was the bluest I'd ever seen, like a picture of Hawaii, and it was surrounded by jagged rock cliffs. It was beautiful. A car horn honked at me, and my attention went back to the road. I saw a parking area and decided to exit the freeway.

I saw a small hamburger stand, restrooms at the bottom of the exit ramp, and so many families milling around that I knew it was safe to stop.

Many people hiked on a smaller mountain, and some of the tourists stood overlooking the top of a cliff. *It must be a spectacular view*, I thought. Something drew me to the top. I just had to see it.

The danger of being on the cliff didn't even bother me as I climbed the short distance up its hill behind another family group. After all, I could become disabled someday, or even tomorrow . . . At least I could always say I climbed a mountain, even if it was a small one.

Signs posted on the trail warned of dangerous terrain at the top. Kids were discouraged from going farther. I wondered whether I should continue up the scrub-covered hill myself, but I pressed on, even though many tourists now turned back. Besides, what did it even matter?

The whole MS thing was a nightmare. I just wanted to forget it.

I'd pretend that I never heard the doctor, that I never heard of MS, that I'd be on my way to New York in March for the company audition. But my pretending didn't work this time. It depressed me further, so I continued climbing the more difficult slope.

Reaching the top, the last of the tourists moved on, and I was alone. I moved out toward the edge to look over and gasped. The mountain was short on one side, but on the other side, the cliff overhung an abyss where the rock face fell to a much lower depth than the hike promised. As I looked over the cliff's edge, the strains of *Swan Lake* returned to haunt me. I imagined my future career disintegrating in front of my eyes. The lights! The blur of the white tulle, floating like a swan across the stage, and then stumbling on pointe. What would I do?

I had to make a decision.

I stared out again at the water below and watched as the waves crashed like the cataclysmic crescendo of the dying swan's last moments. White foam swirled in the water like Cygnus feathers awash in a whirlpool of frenzy, looking more like the drool from a mad dog than a graceful swan demise. I could hear the strains of *Swan Lake*'s dramatic music in my head as the water hit the rocks with such force that it seemed like the world was about to come to an end.

My world.

I stood near the edge of the jagged cliff and looked up into the sky. The waning light of dusk matched my gloom. The wind then whispered to me: "You may never dance."

The cliff was high. The water with the rocks below seemed like a mile down. I had to make a decision. What would I do if I couldn't dance?

Dad ripped my world apart moving me to California, with me gripping onto the 59th Street Bridge in

Manhattan, and him pulling me to the Golden Gate. Feeling stretched across the country like a rubber band, I had tried to adjust.

"Dad, I really tried." My cry pierced the darkness. "I tried, but I still want to dance!" My voice reverberated around the cliff.

"Never!" the breeze answered.

I threw my arms up in port de bras and struck a pose in defiance. A lone figure at the top of the mountain, I rose up onto my toes in my sneakers. *I can do it*, I thought, but then I faltered. The millisecond of swan joy turned to tragic irony as I felt the weakness return in my left leg. The MS mocked me, and at that moment, I hated the world. Everything had been taken from me. I sat down on a rock.

Could I do it anyway? Could I prove the doctor wrong? Dad? Could I prove it to myself? I needed strength, but did I have any left? Maybe the illness wasn't the test after all. Perhaps the test was yet to come . . . yet to come . . .

"There is always hope in possibility," I whispered. The wind blew a heavy gust, and I braced myself. "There is always hope in possibility." I screamed back in anger to the water in front of me.

The wind suddenly unbalanced me, and I almost went over. Backing up with caution, I broke into a run, away from the windy cliff, before the chasm swallowed me up.

Racing toward my car, I locked myself inside and just sat there shivering—not from the cold, but from fear.

Looking at myself in the rearview mirror, I saw reflected in the rectangular piece of glass a girl who was going to live to fight and fight with all her heart to dance.

I let out a huge sigh and leaned back to rest a moment.

As the orange-purple dusk turned into a starry night, I thought about New York City, where my life did a one-eighty, and how I was going to fix it all.

Chapter Twelve

The tourists had gone, and I could see the fires and lights of families camped out in the distance. I started the car and took off for the freeway but pulled over again. Where was I? I stopped to ask directions at a gas station. Dad always told me to do that if I got lost.

Dad! I'd forgotten all about him. I had to call. I was in so much trouble! He'd be worried. What would I say? He'd want to know where I was, and I didn't even know. Why didn't he call before? I took my cell phone out of my purse and saw that it was off. I turned it back on and punched in the numbers. I'd have to lie. I'd say I was with Becca and Troy. No. He might already have called them.

I wouldn't lie. I'd tell the truth. I'd tell him that I took a long drive to cool off. I just wouldn't tell him how long the drive really was.

"Dad?" I spoke into my cell phone. He didn't answer. I stared at my black cell-phone cover that had Manhattan Dance Company painted on it in white. "Dad? I took a long drive. I'll be back soon. I didn't want you to worry." I clicked off the call. At least I left a message. "I hope he didn't call the police," I whispered, and then pulled into another gas station mart, bought a water bottle and some cashews, and got directions from a man who didn't speak English very well.

"You way off," the cashier said. "Take other freeway, then change. Three hours." A three-hour drive! How far did I go? Dad was going to kill me. I paid for the purchase and took off again driving an unknown set of freeways in the dark.

The drive was as scary as I thought it might be. I'd driven over a 158 miles because I was so upset. I had to switch freeways three times and watch the lane changes in the darkness. I made a wrong turn and had to exit and then enter the freeway again, but I guess that gave me more practice. I was trying to be mature and optimistic about it.

I needed to hear human voices, so I turned on the radio and hit a few of the buttons. My hand moved back to the steering wheel again, and I heard the DJ on the radio.

"Coming up, more music that we all enjoy . . ." The sad ballad started and I continued the drive.

There were some straight roads and curvy ones, but I found my path in more ways than one. I was determined to get back home. I was more determined to fight this disease. I was even more determined to get back to New York. I'd do it somehow, with every breath in my body, with every muscle and strength of spirit. I would make it to that audition.

The music on the radio calmed me a little, but the song was haunting. The time ticked away. It was already nine o'clock, and I still had fifty miles to go.

I began to hum with the music to keep my mind off of the drive ahead, Dad's reaction when I got home, and my fatigue from it all. My cell phone rang several times, but I couldn't pick it up. I tried to put it on speaker, but couldn't manage it while driving so I gave up. I knew it was Dad.

How could I tell him that I drove all the way to Big Sur?

When I got home, Dad wasn't mad.

"I got your message," he said, grabbing me in a huge hug, and cried. He was just as upset as I was. I really felt guilty for worrying him like that.

What if I had fallen off the mountain? What would he and Petey have done? I shuddered again, remembering the cliff.

"Go to bed," he said. "We'll talk about it in the morning." He hugged me again.

In the morning, I watched the mobile above me. The ballerina with a ripped-off leg suddenly spoke.

"You're me," she whispered. The figure twirled an odd twirl that bobbed and spun unevenly because of her asymmetrical line. It was a sad sight. My future stared right back at me. Turning, I watched the other ballerina twirl on the mobile, the one with the backward port de bras.

"Petey," I said aloud. "Me and Petey . . . Why didn't I see it before?"

I got up and washed my face and looked at my puffy eyes in the bathroom mirror. No way to disguise this. I'd look bad at school. Maybe I could pretend that I cried over a boy, heartbroken . . . but the truth would be that my heart *was* broken but not over some dumb boy. I thought my life could really be over. How many times had I said that recently? How could I have known that it might really, truly happen? But I wouldn't let it!

Going downstairs, I found Dad sitting at the kitchen table eating breakfast, silent, staring. At first we both didn't talk. Then there was some small talk . . . Then the MS crept into the conversation like a venomous snake.

"While there is no cure," Dad said, "there is treatment, and because you're young, you should respond to the medicine."

"Will it hurt?" My fear surfaced again.

"I dunno. Daily injections will have to start this week." I felt numb. Petey came into the kitchen and sat beside me at the table. I put my arm around him but he pulled away. He was in his "not wanting to be touched" stage again.

Dad finished his scrambled eggs and looked up at me occasionally. It was understood that we would not talk about my long car trip ever again.

⁓

Two days later, in the doctor's office, I sat on the stool instead of the bed. I didn't want to be sick, so I would not act like a sick person. Dad sat on the bed and we waited for the doctor.

The daily injection . . . I had to learn to do it, like those diabetics giving themselves insulin. Like a drug addict in an alley. I stayed home from school for the injection lesson.

It made me nervous and I almost felt like leaving, but then the doctor came in before I could bolt.

"The nurse will teach you how to do the injection," he said. The doctor looked tired, and he didn't seem as sympathetic as he was the other day. It was all just routine for him now. Clinical. That was the word. I was just another patient in his office. "I'll experiment with different medications, which should help your dizziness and balance problem." He paused. "Luckily, they found it in time. We can play with the treatment, readjust if necessary."

"Okay," I mumbled.

"Cheer up. You're young."

"That's what Dad said." The doctor flashed that professional smile again and left. The fact that I was too young to be sick only made me feel worse. Fifteen minutes passed and no nurse appeared. I poked my head outside the exam room and asked.

"Oh, she'll be with you soon," I heard someone say. I sat there for another half hour, then felt sleepy, and almost wanted to crawl up on the patient bed and lie down. Fear of the injection didn't bother me anymore. I was so mad about waiting that I just wanted to get it over with. The nurse opened the door.

"I'm Maria," she said and put down a bottle of medicine and a big needle in a clear plastic package. I thought I was going to faint again like I did at the MRI. "This'll be quick. It's not that hard," she said, unwrapping the needle, which now looked a lot larger and pointier. My muscles tensed.

"Will it hurt?"

"You'll get used to it," the nurse said confidently. "The drug's an injectable interferon."

"Does it have any side effects?" I asked.

"Not as many as some of the others. Don't worry," the nurse answered.

"Great!"

"Just don't inject it too close to physical activity."

I shook my head. "I don't know if I can do this."

Nurse Maria laughed. "Yes, you can. Now, you can put it in your thigh or your arm, beneath the skin. The thigh is the easiest because it goes into the fatty part of the skin." Nurse Maria moved my exam gown up a little to expose the side of my thigh.

"I'll come back when you're finished," Dad said and left the little room looking uncomfortable. Nurse Maria went back to her task.

"Men! They're such chickens," the nurse said and felt my thigh. "You don't seem to have any fat on you anywhere," she said.

"I'm a ballet dancer."

"That explains it. You are nothing but toned muscle. This might hurt a little bit, then." My body leaned back as far away from Nurse Maria as it possibly could. She held the needle and the medicine. "You put the needle into the bottle, fill it up" She indicated a red mark on the medicine. "There's one dose per bottle." She held the needle's point up in the air. "Then you kick it for air bubbles." The nurse clicked the needle lightly, and a small bubble in the middle of the clear liquid vanished. "Make sure that you hit the needle to destroy the air bubbles."

"Why?"

"You don't want an air bubble in your system. It can kill you."

I gasped. "I can't do it." My heart raced wildly. The nurse laughed.

"Yes, you can!" She laughed heartily again, and I wanted to run from the room for her laughing at me like that. My body shook from head to toe. This woman wanted me to inject myself with a lethal needle that could have an air bubble in it, and I couldn't even keep my hands and legs from shaking. Was she crazy? I shook my head violently.

"No. I'll never be able to do that."

The nurse grabbed my shoulders. "You have to. If you want to dance."

"But the doctor said there's no guarantee!"

"There's no guarantee in life in anything," the nurse said. "What would you do if you couldn't become a ballet dancer? What if they didn't think you were good enough?"

"I'd try to do my best," I said weakly.

"Do they hire everyone who ever went to the ballet school?" I had to think about that for a moment. They only chose the top five percent. But I was in the top five percent, wasn't I? At least I was when I was in New York. Here in California now, I wasn't so sure. Tears rushed to my eyes because I didn't know how to answer the nurse's question. "Have you ever thought about something else you want to do in life?" The nurse smiled nicely. "You can't do ballet professionally when you're forty-five."

"The primas do!" I countered, but I knew she was right. The career of a dancer was short. It was about ten years or less. *Kind of like being a model*, I thought. What would I do after the company? It never even occurred to me before. What would I do if I never even got into the company in the first place?

"It's always good to have a backup plan," the nurse said, and I hated her for it, even though I realized she was right. I hated it when grown-ups were right. It gave me a queasy feeling in my stomach.

"I'm not telling anyone," I stated.

"About what?" The nurse paused, waiting for my answer.

"About the multiple sclerosis. Only Dad and I will know."

"There's nothing to be ashamed of, Kendra. And it will take a lot of energy to hide it, but it is your decision." The nurse continued with the medical procedure. "Now, I want you to try it. I'm using a practice solution." The nurse gave me the needle, which shook in my hand. I fingered it gingerly, staring at the point.

"I don't like it when the doctor gives me a needle. I feel scared giving it to myself."

"You'll lose your fear, then." She adjusted my hand on the needle and put hers on top of mine. She guided the needle into the surface layer of the skin on my thigh, and she pushed my thumb to release the solution into my leg. "Did you feel that?" I looked up at her and shook my head no. I didn't feel a thing.

The process of the needle overwhelmed me and I paid no attention to the sting, if there was any. "Now you try it," she said.

"I can't." I gulped. "I feel like a drug addict!" My body cringed, revolted.

"Drug addicts can't dance on pointe, can they?" The nurse leaned closer. "You can do it."

"That's easy for you to say," I said. "You don't have to give yourself a needle every day!" Nurse Maria frowned, put the syringe down, and rolled up her sleeve. There were bruises on her arm and old needle marks. I gasped.

"I'm a diabetic," the nurse said. "I have to give myself a shot of insulin every single day, twice a day." Suddenly I felt foolish and looked down at the floor. "And I live a normal life." The nurse lifted my chin and looked directly into my eyes. "You can do it too." She smiled a little and handed me another syringe. I took it and put the needle and bottle together. The liquid pumped into the needle and I drew it up to the red line on the bottle.

"Oh, good, a bubble," the nurse said. "Now you can practice tapping to get rid of it." I tapped and the air bubble dissolved into the liquid. I silently prayed a quick prayer of thanks. "Good. Now find a spot and pinch your skin." I did it. "Now prick the skin." She guided me with her voice alone this time. ". . . and . . . inject." I pushed and the liquid went into my thigh. A sigh of relief went through my entire being.

"I did it!"

"You sure did."

"Do I take this stuff home?"

"Not yet. You and your Dad will come and practice with me every day for a week. Then we'll have you do it at home. You'll have to keep all this stuff away from Petey," the nurse said. "Keep it on a high shelf and discard it in this bag, which you'll bring back to the office." I sighed again as I took the plastic bag with a toxic waste symbol on it.

"Thanks," I said. The nurse put her hand on my shoulder again.

"You'll be fine."

❧

Later, I thought of the nurse's words: "You'll be fine." It was easy for her to say. She didn't have an audition coming up in March, an audition where you needed fine motor skills. And it was already February.

I threw a glance to the corner of the ballet room to check on Petey. He wasn't there. Panicking, my heart raced, but the girls pointed to the barre. There was Petey with his leg on the wooden barre. My worry about the MS momentarily disappeared when I saw him standing in that position. Not only had Petey left his corner, but he was also trying to imitate us! His left hand held the barre, and he gripped the pink tutu in his free hand. He did funny battements with his inside leg. I went over to him, bent down tenderly, and whispered.

"Petey? You want to do ballet?" He didn't respond but looked straight ahead, absorbed in the dance.

Several girls crowded around, including Becca, who asked, "Did he ever do this before?"

"In New York? No." I shook my head. "He never went to my class in New York." I stepped back to observe him. "We had a regional center aide there. This is the first time he's ever seen a ballet room, here in the school with me. It must be the music . . ."

"Or the movement," Mrs. Cassidy added. I smiled, I think, for the first time in a week, since I heard that awful diagnosis of MS.

"Leave space for Petey," Mrs. Cassidy said, understanding the situation. We resumed class, and Petey "danced" with us. During the center floor practice, Petey still held onto the barre and occasionally threw his leg up. Once, he even bent down in a sweeping port de bras. After the class, Petey wouldn't let go of the barre. He grunted his anger grunt.

"Time to go now, Petey." I tried to pry his fingers from the wooden beam, but he held steadfast, just the way he held onto the Christmas light that broke in his hand. "We'll come back, Petey, tomorrow. I promise." Petey hesitated for a moment, then slowly let go of the barre. He took my hand, because he trusted me.

"That's remarkable," Mrs. Cassidy commented as we left the ballet room. She followed Petey and me out to the car.

"There's something about this place that makes Petey come alive," I said. "Maybe the pumpkins startled him into awareness. The bright orange colors."

Mrs. Cassidy and I looked around.

There were no pumpkins now. I looked out at the vineyard's dead leaves and old vines that blew in the strong February wind, and I eyed the bald pumpkin patches. "It's the inside of the ballet school," I said. "Since I've been bringing him here . . . It's the music. He feels the vibrations and the movement."

"You know, the move from New York to California could have done it as well. A different environment could have expanded his world somehow," Mrs. Cassidy said. Becca and Troy walked up behind their mother.

"I never thought of that." I reflected on Mrs. Cassidy's words for a minute as I put Petey into his car seat. Then I suddenly grabbed the roof of the car, feeling a little woozy.

That dizziness again! I clenched my fist tight and closed my eyes, trying to make the feeling go away. I held my breath, angry, waiting for it all to pass. I felt like I was going to fall down unconscious but fought against it.

The world started to spin and my right leg began to give way. I stiffened my muscles to hold them together, retain my stance, but I could feel the leg going numb. No! I wouldn't let this multiple sclerosis defeat me! I promised myself.

I froze in my position and gripped onto the metal top of the car. It was like being on top of the cliff all over again, where I could fall any second and all would be lost.

All would be lost . . .

For a moment I forgot that Mrs. Cassidy, Becca, and Troy stood beside me. Then I remembered. It embarrassed me to have this spell in front of them, especially when I tried so hard not to tell them about the MS for fear of them pitying me. I wanted them to see me for who I was—an aspiring ballerina.

I grabbed the roof of the car even harder for support. My Spartan mentality emerged.

Endure!

Resist!

Achieve!

It seemed like an eternity to me until the dizziness died down, but it was only seconds. As I held my breath, they all noticed my odd behavior right away.

"Is everything all right, Kendra?" I immediately began to cry.

"No," I trembled and turned to face Mrs. Cassidy.

"What is it?"

I hesitated. I'd vowed to keep the MS private, but it was hard with tears betraying my mask of secrecy. Besides, I had to confide in the Cassidy family. They were so supportive. I just couldn't lie to them, and I needed to let it out myself or I'd simply burst. The nurse was right. It'd take too much energy to keep it quiet, brush off the leg spasms, constantly explain the dizziness

"The doctor says I have multiple sclerosis," I blurted. "I'm taking injections every day. They're supposed to stop my dizziness, but I felt dizzy. Maybe they're not working . . . and my leg is sore and bruised. I didn't know how to tell you." I cried louder now because it was the first time I felt the dizziness since the injections began. I cried because I hadn't told Mrs. Cassidy and Becca and Troy about the MS. I couldn't hold it in any longer.

"Oh, Kendra. You should have told us right away what the doctor said!"

"My ballet career." Momentarily I managed to hold my tears at bay. I looked around and saw that even Petey looked at me, concerned. "What good is it for me to continue ballet if my heart will be broken when I can't do it any longer?" A sob slipped out and my voice was staccato in my throat. I couldn't breathe.

"You keep coming to class," Mrs. Cassidy said. "You need to keep your muscles toned. It will be good therapy for your emotional state as well. Besides . . ." Mrs. Cassidy's tone softened. "We'll be auditioning for the mini company for the spring performance soon. We're doing *Coppélia* again. You'd be perfect for the part of the doll. But only if you practice, and you have to audition like everybody else." Mrs. Cassidy's short blonde hair blew in the wind, and she smiled as she lifted my chin. "Okay?"

Wiping my eyes and nose with my sleeve, I slapped my leg in frustration, but it hurt from the injection. My head nodded and I got into the car. Mrs. Cassidy leaned in the window.

"We all have troubles, Kendra," she said, pushing back her hair "It's how we handle those troubles that makes us champions." I tried to smile and started the car.

❦

When I got home, the numbness in my leg got even worse. I hobbled in the door of the house with Petey.

"Dad?"

"In the kitchen," his voice called out to me.

"Dad, I need help." My voice shook with fear as I held onto the banister near the door. I moved from the glossy wooden banister to the hall table, which I tipped over, and the vase with fake flowers on the table fell and everything crashed—me, the flowers, and the vase, which lay shattered on the hardwood floor. Petey got scared and ran like a gazelle. *I guess he has athletic talent after all*, I thought as I saw him sprint away. Though I'd lost all feeling in my leg by now, for some reason I laughed hysterically. I was terrified. Dad came running and rescued me from amid the splintered porcelain.

"Are you sick?" Dad picked me up and put me down in a living room chair. "What happened?"

"I can't control my leg!"

"The MS?"

I nodded.

"And I feel really dizzy too." Panic gripped me and I began to hyperventilate. "My leg, Dad. I can't stand on it." Dad rubbed my calf muscle with brisk motion.

"You'll get the feeling back again in a minute," he said.

"No, my right calf is numb, like when your muscles fall asleep and you try to step on the floor, and your leg gives way." Dad nodded.

"That's all it is?"

"No. This time it's lasted more than fifteen minutes."

"How did you drive the car? And with Petey?"

"I had enough pressure to push the gas pedal and brake, but then started losing it when I got out of the car."

Dad looked alarmed. "Call me next time, and I will pick you up wherever you are! We're going to see the doctor, right now."

"Without an appointment?"

"Either that or it's the emergency room."

♋︎

"We have to change the medication." Dr. Meyer sat back in his office chair while I fidgeted with my hair. "We'll try some corticosteroids . . . A pill. No more injections, Kendra, at least for now." It didn't make me feel better, especially after he said, "You're having a relapse."

"How long will it last?" Dad asked.

"Could be a few days, a week, a month . . ."

"A month?" I was flabbergasted. "My audition's in a month!" My chest heaved in panic. My eyes searched the doctor's, pleading for his answer.

"I don't know how long the relapse will last," was his response. I felt as if a weight of iron crushed me into the floor.

"Am I really sick? Am I going to die?"

"It'll be all right, Kendra," Dad reassured me.

"We'll try new medicine." The doctor flipped through his file folder.

"Will it help, though? Am I going to die?" No one answered me.

Dad leaned forward, and Petey jumped off his lap

to stare out the window. I watched Petey stare at a bird on a tree again. He pointed, enthralled. I remembered that he was making progress, and I felt devastated that I wasn't too.

"We have to experiment, find the right combination," Dr. Meyer continued. "We'll monitor closely and keep trying until we do." Dr. Meyer tore off a prescription slip. "And, no, you're not going to die, Kendra. Most people with MS don't." Dr. Meyer handed the slip to me.

"Most people?" I whispered.

The relapse didn't last for just a few days, or even just a week. It lasted for nine whole days. It had been nine very long days since I could go to ballet or even to Seneca High. Becca emailed me the homework assignments, but they just sat there in my inbox. I ignored them. How could I do homework at a time like this? What if I only had a short time to live? Would homework even matter?

"Homework does matter," Dad admonished me.

I fingered my binder on the couch, but the thought of writing an essay on Dickens's *A Tale of Two Cities* made me feel worse. All I could do was look at the little white bottle of pills on top of the TV. I shook them and heard the medication dance around inside like jumping beans, the magic beans that might get me well. I had already taken them for over a week and nothing. My foot was still numb. I couldn't even point it.

"I hope this one works," I said, only half joking, and took one pill out and downed it with a sports drink. Dad looked over at me from his recliner and made a stern face. "Well, at least it's not the injection needle of death," I said.

Unfortunately, the joke fell flat. I was bored. Trying to stretch my leg and do some beats with my feet, my numb leg didn't respond. I couldn't control my muscle. It scared me; I mean, it really scared me not to be in control of my own body.

The dialogue of *The Red Shoes* in the background on the TV made me look up. The girl on screen, Victoria Page, ascended a stairway to glory, like a princess about to get the big part. I knew the story by heart. I turned the sound on mute and just stared at the TV.

Dad looked up, concerned. "Haven't you watched that movie enough?"

"What if I never go back to normal? What if I really can't do ballet? Manhattan Dance might never hire me because of the multiple sclerosis." I voiced my thoughts aloud and Dad looked over at me.

"It's a real possibility, honey. If you sign a contract, they'll want to know that you are fit to dance. They'd have to depend on your ability to perform on cue. Otherwise . . ." Dad didn't finish his sentence. He knew how devastating it was for me. He went back to reading his paper, and I sunk into nothingness again, wondering about my future at Manhattan Dance.

Petey grunted, breaking my thoughts, and I glanced over at him sitting on the sofa. He looked so tiny. He still weighed only forty-five pounds. He looked so thin as he sat there, but he could have the strength of ten men when he had a tantrum. Only this time he didn't have a tantrum. I threw a smile over to Petey, but he had a flat effect once more with no further response.

"He noticed a bird again today," I said. "It's the third or fourth time."

"It's a fluke," Dad answered from his old recliner. "You've been crying? Your eyes look red."

"No," I lied. I didn't want Dad to think I was a baby, especially since I'd been acting like one ever since we moved from New York. I'd cried earlier in the afternoon and then fell asleep from fatigue. I knew that I was more mature than this. Dad said that the disease forced me to be more of an adult earlier, but the disease made me emotionally regress somehow. I felt like someone who needed her mommy to bring chicken soup and make a fuss over her in bed with the thermometer and play cards to keep her company. I wanted that. I missed my mom terribly.

"You'll be back to normal again soon, Kendra." Dad was so reassuring, but I wished that I could have believed him.

"Yeah," I said halfheartedly. I got up from the couch and jumped on one foot over to Dad like some kind of goofy rabbit.

"You're getting kind of good with that hop." Dad smiled.

"Let's hope it's not permanent," I answered, but I suddenly worried about that too. That overpowering feeling of dread overcame me. The words I tried to hide from Dad slipped out. "Do you think I'll be . . . disabled?"

"We have to be optimistic, Kendra."

I nodded. "What if I can't dance?" My voice quivered.

"We'll come to that crossroad when . . . if it happens."

"And what about school? What if I need a wheelchair?"

"You could always do school online." Dad sighed. "Whatever happens, I'll be there with you, but I think you'll be fine."

I finally reached Dad on his recliner.

"Can you promise that?" I wanted him to tell me it would be all right. I needed it. My future depended on it.

Dad scratched his head, uncertain. He didn't know what to say. I wanted an answer, but the answer he gave me didn't help.

"The doctor called today. Said there's a support group for teens with MS that meets once a month. I think it's a good idea, hon."

"I'm not going to any support group like I'm some sort of alcoholic!" I shuddered.

"Okay. You don't have to do it. Just think about it."

I changed the subject. "Dad, I wish you'd listen when I tell you about Petey saying 'choc,' Dad, and he responded to the ballet and to the music. We've got to get him a regional center doctor to reassess him."

"Look at you, Kendra. You're dealing with your own illness and you're worried about your brother." Dad smiled. "That's why you're my daughter," he said, and he put his arm around me. "But as for Petey . . . he's autistic. Oh, Kendra, I'd love to see a light in his eyes. He may react once in a blue moon, but he'll always be autistic. I wish it weren't true, but it is."

"No! Dad, he's responding! He *is*." Just then the doorbell rang and Dad got up to answer it.

"Kendra? It's Troy."

"Troy?" My mind went right to my hair. I hadn't even combed it this morning. I ran my fingers through the brown, curly mess and gulped. It bothered me that I looked bad. And it bothered me that I cared that I looked bad in front of Troy. What was wrong with me? I had no romantic ambitions. Ballet and romance could not survive together.

Troy stepped inside before I could think it all out, and stared, probably at my bed-rumpled hair.

"Here," he said and handed me a yellow daffodil and a stack of dance magazines. "Mom wanted to know if you were better." He looked down, then back up. "Are you better?"

"No." Now I looked down at the floor.

Troy walked over to me and took me by the hand. He led me outside to the front steps, and we sat down to look at the sun setting through the tree branches of the California winter.

"What did the doctor say?" Troy looked at me with his intense blue eyes, which showed concern.

"He says I have to wait out the relapse." I looked over again at the sunset. "The doctor says that I'll be better when I'm better."

"That's doctor gobbledygook," Troy said, then laughed a little. "Nobody can keep you down, Kendra. Not the doctor and not the MS. You're obsessed, remember?"

"I hope you're right." My head drooped and Troy lifted my chin.

"I am right. You're a fighter, Kendy." My heart warmed over, and I felt a little guilt for disliking Troy. His hand then touched my cheek and he smiled. His silly grin was contagious, and I felt some butterflies flutter around my stomach. No, they were more like fairies creating little lights inside of me. I tried to quiet them down, but it felt good to smile again. I stared at Troy's face, and all of his bravado disappeared, making him a genuine human being for once. Besides, he called me Kendy and he brought me a flower, which I held up. "Thanks," I said.

"For what?"

"For coming over." Troy looked into my eyes again, stared for a few seconds, then suddenly stood up, nervous.

"What's wrong?" Did I say the wrong thing?

"I was just passing by."

"What do you mean?"

"Gotta go," Troy said and looked away, but not before I saw his face turn crimson.

"But we were just talking . . ."

Troy touched his own cheek like it was hot. He seemed restless. "Basketball's on TV."

"Oh, I can talk basketball," I lied. I didn't want him to leave. He was the first friend I'd talked to in person in nine days. Troy turned back toward me.

"What do you know about basketball?" He stood with arms crossed in a challenge, waiting for my answer.

"Um . . ." I searched my mind quickly for a response. Panicking, my mind went blank, then I tossed out the only thing that I could think of. "I know a bank shot, and there's a guard, and . . . Larry Haynes. My Dad liked him."

Troy stared at me for a moment and then howled with laughter. He laughed so much, his face was redder than an apple.

"Larry Haynes played baseball." He laughed again. "But I'm watching basketball tonight. See ya." Troy turned to go.

"No, you can't miss basketball," I said in a monotone.

"I gotta go," he repeated as if he was asking permission to bolt. I wanted him to stay. "You know, your hair looks bigger." Troy stared at me. "Without the bun you wear all the time."

Oh my gosh! He noticed my hair! All of the fairies and butterflies disappeared, and I could see only a flash of red before my eyes.

"Gooooo!" I countered, and threw the stack of magazines down on the steps. Troy smiled oddly before he took off. He got into his mother's blue car and drove off like a NASCAR racer.

Hobbling into the house in tears, I awkwardly managed the steps to the second floor. Reaching my bedroom, I threw myself on my bed. The daffodil was still in my hand, and I fingered the stem for a moment. Then I threw it to the floor where it lay like some old movie tribute to heartbreak.

My pointe shoes lay on top of my dresser, just waiting for me to make them pirouette. A bottle of pills sat next to them. I glanced over at the laptop on my pillow. Opening it, I saw the image of my last Internet search—treatment for MS.

Why was I so upset about Troy? He didn't really do anything. He came over to see me . . . Why did I care about any of it anyway? Any sort of romantic notion, if that's what it was, made me lose focus on dance. And that was not going to happen!

The computer screen beckoned, and so I looked up more symptoms and treatments for MS. Even though it seemed useless, I also checked my email, still hoping in vain for Miss Irina's response. I told myself that it had gotten lost in cyberspace, but I really couldn't lie to myself any more.

As I typed more and more into the search engine and read everything in sight about multiple sclerosis, I wondered how long the treatment would take . . . A few years? Forever?

Dr. Meyer was right. There were some success stories, but there seemed to be piles upon piles of depressing stories too. People did lead normal lives with treatment, and people also had horrible, disabled lives. It was a crapshoot, just like he said.

You think doctors know everything, and then you find out that they don't. You think parents are supposed to protect you, but sometimes they can't.

Chapter Thirteen

It was three in the morning, and I still I searched the Internet. Another story came up about a woman in her forties; it was really sad, and it depressed me more. Seeing as I was a glutton for punishment, I opened up my email and typed a long newsy message to Liz, my former BFF in New York. I wrote all about my MS, all about my feelings.

The email sat there. I stared at the words on the screen, unable to push the send button. Liz wasn't a friend anymore, and I didn't want to tell anyone in New York about the MS. I wanted to keep it all inside. Just me and Dad and the Cassidys. No one else had to know. So I deleted Liz's email and turned off my bedroom lamp.

Then I remembered Mrs. Cassidy's words. *"It's how we handle those troubles that makes us champions . . ."* Besides, I had hope, didn't I? I took medicine that I had stuck myself with every day for a month. I had pills now. It would make me better. Wouldn't it?

I stared out into space, but fear returned, and my eyes searched the darkness for answers. The darkness didn't answer back, though; it only enveloped me like a cloak of doom.

The next day I did feel better. Dad got tickets to see the Napa Valley Ballet at the little opera house there. "It'll almost be like going to the Met," he joked. "I hear Napa Valley has a lot of culture—symphony, opera, theater, and dance . . ."

I shrugged, still thinking about last night's Internet search, but I kind of started to look forward to the ballet performance, any ballet performance. In an odd way, it was an adventure, like going to the opera house in the middle of the Amazon. In Napa Valley, I'd be going to the ballet in the middle of fields of grapes. No doubt they'd have farmers playing in the orchestra.

"It's black tie," Dad said, and suddenly, it seemed more interesting. I'd get to wear my fancy black gown, the one I wore to see Liz dance in the opera *La Gioconda*, so I agreed.

Later that night, Dad called up the stairs for me.

"Are you ready yet?"

"Almost!" I finished my makeup in the bedroom mirror and took one last look at myself. The black dress was gorgeous. It was perfect. Its ballet bodice top shimmered with small black beads, and the full, black ball gown skirt made me feel like a princess. Any occasion was an excuse to wear it. The skirt twirled as I turned a few chassés near the wall mirror in my bedroom, but my leg was still numb. My hair was perfect, though, except for a stray wisp that just wouldn't stay in place with spray, mousse, or gel. Still, I felt great. It was like the real Kendra was back. I grabbed my little black purse and floated down the stairs.

"You're in your element, Kendra." Dad smiled. He was right. No more pumpkin picking for me. I was a New York girl again now.

"You look good too," I admitted. Dad wore black tie with elegance as he stood by the stairs.

"I promised your mom that I would keep culture in your life," he said. Dad didn't like these things, I knew, but he was doing it for Mom. She had been full of culture, and he knew I had to experience it. So, Dad took me to every gala for every ballet company that was rooted in New York and every ballet company that ever visited. I saw the Kirov and the Bolshoi and the Cuban ballet.

"You look gorgeous!" Becca stood downstairs with Petey. She was babysitting, but would spend the night for a sleepover after I got home so we could talk about the ballet performance. "Gorgeous!" she repeated.

"I wish you were going too." I hugged Becca.

"My company offered me only two tickets last minute, or else I would have taken you," Dad said. "Next time I will," he promised.

"Gotta take a picture for Troy." Becca whipped out her cell phone.

"Wait! My hair!" I tried to tame the unruly wisp and felt nervous that Troy, the Olympian god, would see my picture. Why did I have butterflies in my stomach? Troy never asked me out or anything. Ballet was my future anyway, and no guy would get in the way of that. I liked Troy as a friend, despite his cute bravado. Right? But then, why did I care about him seeing my hair out of place in the photo?

The flash of the camera hurt my eyes momentarily, but I leaned over to see the photo. "Ohhhhh!" Becca and I squealed with laughter. It was a great picture. Becca sent it immediately to Troy, who texted back:

"You look like an angel, Kendra."

"Not the response I expected from him," Becca said sarcastically. "He must be sick."

"An angel," I repeated, and wondered again if I'd hurt Troy's feelings that night in the Mexican restaurant. Suddenly, I felt sad. If I did hurt him, I regretted it deeply.

⟨⟩

The little opera house turned out to be a good-sized opera house. They had balconies and everything. The inside of the theater was gold from its walls to its ceilings. They were really serious about their performances in Napa Valley.

Dad and I took a seat in the orchestra, although he said that the first or second row of the first ring was the place to view ballet. I didn't care. I was up close. We were going to see a few ballet excerpts, which included *Les Sylphides*, *Rodeo*, the *Sugar Plum Fairy pas de deux* from *The Nutcracker*, *Les Patineurs*, which simulated ice skating on stage, and *Giselle*. There were some eclectic modern pieces as well. I could hardly stand the anticipation.

"Are you excited?" Dad asked.

"Yes," I replied with a grin. "I can't wait!" I'd already read the program from cover to cover, but then read it all over again, as if new information would pop up. I stared at the Gala's title, "An Evening to Remember," and I hoped that my name would someday be in a professional program too. Again, I read the biographies of the dancers and the choreographers, eating it all up. I even read the boring advertisements.

The lights dimmed, and the orchestra started. A thrill went up my back. My leg still felt a little numb. It was a reminder of my dark obstacle, but the strains of the orchestra brought me back to life again. The orchestra warm-up always made it seem like magic was going to happen, and it felt that way tonight. The curtain rose and I wanted to fall onto the stage to dance with them all.

The first ballet began. The dancers in *Les Sylphides* were so beautiful in their white tulle. Their swan-like movement made me visualize myself in the corps. Tears formed in my eyes and I had to wipe them away.

"Are you all right?" Dad looked concerned, but I nodded and went back to the performance on stage.

The next piece was *Rodeo*, with its spirited, bucking moves. I enjoyed the Agnes de Mille choreography, but preferred the more feminine, classical ballets that followed.

When the Sugar Plum Fairy and her prince emerged for the pas de deux, tears escaped again from my eyes, though I tried hard to contain them. I saw the star of the San Francisco Ballet performing the part I dreamed of dancing and realized that I might never get the chance to do it. I'd be lucky to be in the corps de ballet, have a featured solo. To reach the status of that Sugar Plum Fairy role, you had to be perfect, and because of the multiple sclerosis I was less than perfect. Suddenly the star performance I had looked forward to all evening shattered all around me.

I wanted to go home.

At intermission I felt better as I walked around the marbled lobby trimmed with gold. I took it all in just in case I might never get to return if I got sicker. I looked at the chandeliers that hung above. On the wall, photos of dancers mesmerized me. The buzz of intermission talk and laughter echoed in my ears. It was happiness that surrounded me, so why did I feel so devastated?

Dad talked to a few of his coworkers and they inspected bottles from some of the local wineries. I noticed a bottle of Academy of the Fields champagne among them. I made a note to remember to tell Becca and Mrs. Cassidy. All the adults stood around talking about the forbidden fruit, and Dad gave me a soda with a cherry.

As I walked around, I saw the distinguished man who sat next to me standing at the other end of the reception hall. The man nodded his head in greeting when he saw me and smiled. It creeped me out, so I walked back with Dad into the theater, hoping that the man wouldn't return, but he sat down next to me again. I moved closer to Dad in my seat.

The lights dimmed quickly, signaling the second act. The buzz of conversation ended and the orchestra started up its introduction into *Les Patineurs*. I settled back in to watch and dream, and the whole gala was over before I knew it.

After the performance, Dad's coworkers wanted to talk to him some more, so they invited us to a late night supper at an expensive restaurant nearby. I was hungry by that time, but I really wanted to go back home to talk to Becca, to tell her how the Sugar Plum Fairy did an exquisite job, how the opera house looked, and about how the Academy of the Fields wine was being sold at intermission. I wanted to tell her about the ballerinas from the San Francisco Ballet and their credits in the program. I had to admit that Napa Valley was like a little New York, in its own way. I texted Becca until Dad told me to put my cell phone away at the table and be polite.

The restaurant was elegant in a rustic way. We sat at a long wooden table with candlelight in the dark, and there were barrels of wine on the opposite wall. The candles gave the room a cozy glow, with the wine and the wooden table and the gray stone walls. There was a lot of ivy near the window and I could see it in the moonlight, creeping along the edges outside the panes.

I ordered a steak but ate a lot of the salad instead. Even though Dad's coworkers were nice and tried to include me, I was bored hearing the grown-ups talk about computer programs and app creation.

After dinner they asked us if we wanted to take the winery tour. Dad said yes and I went along. We walked from the restaurant to a building outside. It looked like a great stone barn with two large wooden doors. The owner opened the doors and we entered to see bottling machinery on one side of a great warehouse and cartons of empty wine bottles on the other, with vats of harvested fruit waiting to be turned into wine. Bored, I decided to text Becca, but Dad shot me a look.

"When we harvest," the winery owner said, "we must first separate the stems from the fruit, then, depending on the type of wine we make, we decide whether to use the skin of the fruit or just the inside pulp. We have a question from Mr. Austin, was it?" I turned to see the conservative man from our table. Looking at him more closely, he seemed like a grown-up version of Rafe.

"Yes, I'm William Austin." The name made me do a double take. "How long do you age the wine?" he asked.

I lost track of the wine talk and stared at Mr. Austin. He looked almost identical to Rafe. It had to be Rafe's father. Was Rafe here too? I looked around but didn't see Rafe anywhere. The tour moved on.

The wine process was interesting, but all I really wanted to do was go home and share it all with Becca. She'd be waiting up for me, and Dad kept us much later than I planned. I looked gorgeous when I left the house, but I felt like a wilted flower on the way home and fell asleep in the car.

When we got home, I found Becca asleep on the couch with the TV remote still in her hand. The television played a movie, but she was out cold. I woke her up and brought her upstairs.

"How many fouettés did they do?" Becca asked, but she fell asleep again on the pillow before I could answer.

Funny. As I lay in bed yawning, I thought about how the musicians in the Napa Valley ballet orchestra weren't really farmers after all. They were really good.

The music from the ballet still floated through my mind two days later in school. It made an overcast Monday seem sunnier as it drifted through my algebra equations in math, carried me away to nirvana in world history and made me feel literary in English as I wrote about dancers.

The music in my head stopped, though, as I neared the cafeteria.

My protein bar was little comfort as I drank a water bottle. I looked around the cafeteria only to realize that I really was more of an outsider than I thought. Classical music from the ballet made me happy, but the other kids wouldn't understand that, especially Bailey Adams, the mean girl, who sat with her cheerleader friends at a table on the other side of the room.

As I watched the others having fun at lunch, I remembered Madison School for Girls, where the "Vocals" sang at lunchtime, where everyone did an art, and nobody laughed at anybody, except sometimes an off-key violin quartet. No one ever laughed because we were all the same. But I wasn't at Madison School for Girls anymore. I was at Seneca High with over a thousand students, and except for Becca and Troy, nobody liked anything that I did. I began to wonder if I should pretend that I didn't like any of this culture stuff. Maybe that was the key to assimilation. Pretend not to be yourself.

"What's wrong?" I turned. Sylvan stood beside me. She was wearing the same black tee-and-skirt outfit, except for the flower in her hair, which was yellow.

"Nothing," I said and bit a small morsel off my protein bar. "Why?"

"You were very . . . pensive," Sylvan remarked. I sighed. *I should talk to Sylvan*, I thought. She always made the effort to talk to me, and she wasn't the kind to blab things around. I decided to trust her. I also realized that Sylvan wouldn't laugh at me too.

"I don't think I fit in," I said.

"Join the club," she answered and sat down. "Oh, and don't talk to me, or you'll really be a social outcast." She laughed, and I smiled a little.

"Yeah, but maybe I should pretend that I don't like ballet and classical music, you know?" I took another bite of my protein bar and gulped some water out of anxiety.

"But it's who you are," Sylvan said. "I told you before. You can't hide what you are inside. Besides," she continued, "they would eventually find out anyway, right?" She smiled a little, patted my hand, and then left me at the table with my empty water bottle, a protein bar wrapper, and deep thoughts about myself.

༄

After school, I dropped off my review of the Napa Valley Ballet to the *Seneca 'Zine*. This time, we didn't have to use the science lab. The renovation was finished and we had a real little newspaper office. It was almost the size of a closet, but it fit two desks, a computer, a printer, a phone, and two chairs.

"Review something good, you said, so I did," I said proudly. Rafe Austin took my review of the Napa Valley Ballet's "An Evening to Remember," and read it.

"The gala!" My choice of performance apparently impressed him. "You were there?" He took his glasses off and skimmed my article. "It's good. You know there's a lot of culture here in Napa Valley. Even if the teens at school don't like it, they should. It would broaden their horizons."

"Do you really believe that?" I asked.

"No, but I have to say stuff like that as editor." He looked at me directly. "Besides, my father's on the Arts Council." He smiled proudly and looked at my article again. "I said

you'd write an arts column. You need to give it a name." I
thought about Sylvan's words just minutes before, and then
blurted it out.

"*Reviews by Opera Girl,*" I said without hesitation, and
Rafe laughed. He'd obviously heard my nickname around
school. "I'm serious," I said. "It's who I am."

"I thought you were a ballet dancer." Rafe put the review
down on his editor's desk.

"I am. But I've gone to all kinds of performances. Everyone does in New York." I paused. "Since I've been here, I've
been hiding, but why should I hide what I am? Who I am?"

Sylvan was right. The other kids would find out. I'd
make a slip in conversation, stretch my leg in ballet position under my desk, or the teacher might even make me
read my composition about dancers in front of the class.

Rafe thought about it for a moment and agreed. "It
might make for some good publicity," he commented.
"Reviews by Opera Girl," he repeated the name. "Sounds
good, actually."

"I also did a review on the band concert." I handed him
a second paper. "Use whatever you want. I could review
the college fair next week as well." Rafe brightened at this.

"You're a go-getter. I thought you were really shy." He
sat back and smiled, then his face blushed red.

"Being shy doesn't mean you can't do it." I felt defen-
sive and looked down. I hated being shy. It was always a
struggle with myself and other people.

"I know," Rafe said quickly, then stopped himself,
and put his head down again. I felt even shyer now that
I bared my soul to Rafe, and didn't want to talk about
it anymore.

"Besides, I already wrote a scathing article on the cafeteria. I'll do a thorough job on the college fair too, if you let me." His face went crimson again. It almost seemed like he was going to ask me something, but then didn't.

"Go for it!" He seemed a little disappointed for some reason and looked away.

❧

I wanted to write up a storm. I felt inspired by my articles. Rafe liked them and they were really going to be published in the 'Zine. The next day I had another doctor's appointment, so I took my laptop with me. It was always a long wait, so I decided to try to knock one review out rather than waste my time reading worn fashion magazines touched by other sick people. Besides, it was a routine visit. I had nothing to fear. The handle on the door moved and Dr. Meyer came in with my chart.

"Good morning, Kendra."

I nodded. The fear always crept in when I saw the doctor. "Everything's fine," I said immediately.

"But you told me you have numbness. That's not good. We'll have to change that," he said and flashed his professional smile. "How are you doing with the medication?"

"Fine," I responded.

"And your feet, any numbness there?" he asked as he felt my left foot, then my right.

"No." My short answers didn't answer his questions well, and I thought about them as I sat on the cold paper on the exam room bed. Once again, I crinkled as I fidgeted.

"We'll try an intramuscular shot with a new medication."

"Another shot? What does it do? "

"It targets the immune system that is attacking the myelin."

"What's myelin?"

"The myelin is a sheath surrounding the nerves in the brain and spinal cord. The medicine will try to prevent it from damaging—"

"So, it interferes with the MS."

The doctor laughed. "You're right." He smiled. "Anyway, it should offset the numbness. If it doesn't, well . . ." He hesitated. "We'll be hopeful."

Hopeful? "What do you mean?" The doctor smiled again, a little nervous.

"Nothing. I used the wrong word. Sorry," he said and left. Nurse Maria was off today, so Nurse Andrea came in with my new medicine. She handed it to me in a plastic bag, and I exchanged it for an old white plastic bag of toxins I had neglected to hand in from before, along with empty medicine bottles from the last few months.

"Thanks," I said and left.

⤝⋅⋅⤞

Back at school, students laughed riotously as I walked down the hallway to my dreaded Algebra II class. When I saw two boys reading the *Seneca 'Zine* on their cell phones, I realized that I made a terrible mistake. I thought the sarcasm of the column name "Opera Girl" would calm the taunting, that I'd be laughing with them, but now all I heard were snickers and howling as I walked the halls of Seneca High. I wanted to disappear.

A big belly laugh emanated from a boy nearby and a bunch of girls in a group broke into hilarious laughter. I closed my eyes as I walked along the hall and just wanted to die.

"Way to go, *Opera Girl*," a boy shouted to me.

"Oh no!" It was one of the fat kids everybody made fun of. I tried to turn my head away, but he jumped in front of me to ensure that I saw him. He flipped two thumbs up.

"The mystery meat in the burgers is like corrugated cardboard," he said, hamming it up, "between two hard white bricks of bread. I almost broke my teeth!" He howled.

Bailey Adams, queen bee, held court farther down the hall and also asked one of her sycophants to read.

"It's about time somebody complained officially," the follower said. Bailey glanced over at me and our eyes locked. She then screwed up her mouth a little and turned her head away again, avoiding my stare. She grabbed the paper back from her friend and read.

"Every item of food is a disgusting version of the original, but the sum of the parts make up the whole (menu, that is) which is unhealthy, unappealing, and actually inhibits the academic performance of the students. The breaded mystery meat on Monday turned out to be country fried steak, which was paired with overcooked baked beans, mushy apple slices, underdone white rice, and creamed corn. Aside from the dubious nutritional value of the lunch, it was totally without presentation and was an affront to the community of Apple Glen. Tuesday was no better, with heart-clogging mac and cheese, which looked like it was upchucked onto the plate."

The sycophant girls laughed, but Bailey was not amused.

"Upchuck? How rude," she commented. She looked over at me again to see if I was still there. I was. It was kind of funny to see her read my article, so I waited around just to make her feel as uncomfortable as she had made me on my first day.

"No way!" a football player said. "Upchucked onto the plate?" He grabbed the *'Zine* from Bailey and she left in a huff, but her friends stayed to hear the football player read the rest of the article.

". . . I could tell you the menu for the rest of the week; however, it was just more of the same, a mix of hash with no basis in protein at all, overloaded with enough carbohydrates to last for three days of meals, and a sugar content that the American Dental Association would prohibit . . . The facts for this article were checked and rechecked in the lab by the Seneca High School science club."

"Way to go, nerds!" the football player shouted and continued reading as even more students crowded around him.

"I am putting out a 'call to action' to the Seneca High School administration to remedy this problem," I said. "I have included a petition for the students to sign and it's posted on the door of the *Seneca 'Zine* office."

I approached and took the magazine away from the football player, but I didn't read it. I had it memorized.

"We live in one of the richest parts of the country," I said, "not in money, but in agriculture. If we can grow the best crops and make the best grapes for the best wines, why can't our high school have a healthier menu?"

"Way to go, Opera Girl!" the boy yelled again, and the others yahooed.

"Who'll sign the petition?" I waved the *'Zine* in the air, and a plethora of hands rose up. "That way!" I pointed, and a rush of kids fell over one another laughing to sign the paper on the *'Zine* door. It was then I realized that the kids were not laughing at me, but with me.

"They liked the article." It was Rafe behind me now.

He opened his mouth to say something again, but then didn't. I watched him walk away. What was he trying to say to me?

Becca waited for me outside to take the school bus. Dad had decided it might be better for me not to drive the long distance to school for a while, until I got a clean bill of health from the doctor. I still drove to ballet because it wasn't as far. Besides, I liked the camaraderie of the bus with Becca and Troy.

"What a great article!" Becca blurted out as she boarded with me right behind her.

"Thanks. Only the school will read it though," I reminded her, as we took a seat.

"No!" Becca was excited. "The local paper is interested in our food fight. They want to print a headline: 'Land of Agriculture Serves Low Quality Cardboard Meals to Its Children.'"

"You're kidding?"

"She's serious." Rafe jumped on the yellow bus and took a seat nearby. "I just got the call from the Napa Valley Gazette. It's spreading like wildfire around the school. And you"—Rafe smiled—"are the reason. Our 'Zine will get a journalism award for this one, and so will you! I predict it."

Troy fell onto the bus, pushed by a track buddy. He grabbed a seat nearby, but he was all sweaty, and we pulled back. "What'd I miss?"

"Only that Kendra may win an award is all," Becca said in the seat behind me, "for her sharp, investigative journalism."

"Oh." Troy turned to talk to his track buddy about the

meet. Rafe changed his seat beside me. Troy looked at me and then stared out the window, his face hot and red.

"My father's the chairman of the debut of a teen cellist. She's a female Yo-Yo Ma," Rafe said. "The concert is in a private room at the opera house, and I have an extra ticket. Do you want to go?"

"You and me?" My breath stopped for a moment, and I could see Troy look over at us. Rafe nodded.

"You're the only person I know who'd appreciate it." Rafe smiled, and this time he didn't look away. Wow. Was Rafe asking me out?

"I'd love it," I responded. "When is it?" Troy shot up from his seat and came over.

"She can't go. She has ballet." Troy surprised me as he stood balancing himself on the floor of the rickety school bus. Rafe looked up at him.

"Who are you, her father?" I worried that Troy might get aggressive, so I changed the subject.

"Wow! Did the Seneca Lions destroy Miller High, or what?" I threw it out there, hoping that Troy would fall into talk about football, but unfortunately, he challenged Rafe instead.

"When is it?" Rafe looked up at Troy, who loomed over him in size and attitude, so Rafe gulped.

"Saturday night," Rafe said uneasily, "and what business is it of yours, Troy?"

"She has her audition to think about," Troy responded. "She can't overtire herself."

"It's okay, Troy. It'll only be one night." I looked back at Rafe. "Troy's my big brother watching out for me." Troy's face went blank, and he threw himself back into his seat and stared out the window again. His face became hot and red once more. Becca tried to talk to him, but he waved her off.

I blushed a little too. I just got asked out on a date, so I should have been happy. Instead, I felt terrible because I might have hurt Troy's feelings again, and I wasn't sure exactly why.

For a moment I forgot I was sick. As the ramshackle bus road along Chapel Street, I felt like I fit in. But there was a problem: Rafe and Troy were like oil and water.

Chapter Fourteen

That night I still felt terrible about Troy, but I decided to make dinner for Dad to get it out of my mind. Besides, Dad needed a break. I nuked a frozen bag dinner of fettuccine Alfredo, but I got creative and added some small tomato wedges around the pasta. Then I made a thin line of black pepper around the white plates' edges, just the way they do in the restaurants. It looked sort of professional. In places, the pepper was lopsided, but it looked nice.

Dad entered the kitchen behind me.

"What's this?" He sat down at the table, already set with the plates of pasta with their wavy-lined, black-pepper edges. Petey sat at the table too. He picked at the yellow-white pasta with his hands.

"Sit down. It will get cold," I said and began eating. My plate contained only half the amount of pasta.

"What a surprise this is!" Dad said with a mouthful of food. "It's good," he said between bites.

"You're not the only king of frozen food," I said.

"I pass the crown," he said, smiling.

"I thought you'd be late, but you got here just in time." I pushed some pasta aside.

"I'm late tonight because we're now working on cell-phone apps. We had a long, long meeting." Dad yawned. "How was school?"

"I made a hit with my biting article on the cafeteria."

"Biting, eh? That a pun?"

I laughed. "And I got a date for Saturday night."

Dad's ears perked right up. "With who?"

"You'd like him, Dad. His father's on the Wine Country Arts Council." Dad approved not only of the date but also of my fettuccine. I heard Petey grunt and saw him eating his pasta by himself. It was all over his face, but he kept going, and he even looked over at Dad and me and scrunched his right eye.

⚬ℓℓ℺

The next day, ballet class was grueling. My muscles weren't cooperating and my turn-out was off. Perhaps the muscles cramps hadn't gone away completely. Maybe they were hibernating in small tendons and joints that made my natural turn-out harder to achieve for some reason.

At the barre, I pushed myself and began frappés on the left, then on the right. Petey wasn't on his usual little chair. He was twirling round and round, grunting.

"Sit down, Petey," I whispered, and he stopped. He didn't sit down, but rather stared at me with big brown eyes that seemed almost vacant. Mrs. Cassidy moved him back toward his little chair in the corner of the room, and he obediently sat once more, wooden like Pinocchio. I turned my attention back to the barre. We had just switched to petite battements and I caught a glimpse of Petey moving around again. When I turned my head, he was standing, staring. We advanced onto grande battements near the end of the barre work. Then I heard giggling from the other girls and looked around. Becca motioned to me and pointed. Petey was at the barre, oblivious to the others, lost in his own world. He kicked his leg up and down, out of sync with the music, but made a decent impression of a battement. I was astonished.

"He's responding," I whispered.

Mrs. Cassidy called for the end of the barre and we went to the center floor. Petey stayed at the barre and lifted his leg.

"Fifth position," Ms. Cassidy called out, and we all scurried, ready to begin the center floor combination. As we began the combination, I saw Petey raise his arm in a funny, angular port de bras.

"Tendu croisé . . . close plié . . . développé to arabesque . . . close fifth. Fondu . . . plié . . . fourth to double pirouette . . ." Mrs. Cassidy called out the moves, but I heard only every other word or so. I knew the combination by heart, so I looked over at Petey again while dancing. He never once looked down at his leg doing battement, but he stared straight ahead. He performed the movements dutifully, like a little wooden ballet soldier. From the expression on his face, I could tell it was serious business.

". . . Fouetté en dehors . . . keep it going . . . keep it going . . . and . . . close!" Mrs. Cassidy waved her hands.

"On the diagonal . . . Piqué, piqué, three chassés and grand jeté . . ."

"Maybe I have a new pupil," Mrs. Cassidy murmured as she walked by me, waiting in line on the diagonal. She winked.

The center floor continued with increasing difficulty. My pointe shoes, though, were in that perfect stage—broken in just right, with newer and better toe pads. My toes were taped in just the perfect places, and the shoes' peach, satin exterior was still pristine for elite swan-like presentation. I danced well after the tedious barre work. I soared through the jumps and turned sharply. "Crisp," as Miss Irina used to say, "like chip!" I suddenly felt sad at the thought of Miss Irina, but Mrs. Cassidy's voice kept me going.

"Balancé, balancé . . . en pointe . . . raise to arabesque . . . hold . . . one, two, three, four . . ." Some of the girls fell off their pointe after the first two counts, but I was determined to keep it as long as I could. ". . . five . . ." I caved and came down with a thud. ". . . and . . . close." Mrs. Cassidy laughed a little. "You almost made it to six," she said.

I stared at Petey again, and he persevered with his leg movements. His little leg was getting tired, I could see, as he lifted it lower and lower each time, yet he didn't stop.

"Would you look at that?" Mrs. Cassidy touched her forehead in amazement.

❧

That night, I asked Petey to repeat the battements at home. Petey obediently threw his leg up in the air to the music of the radio.

Dad took it all in and almost looked like he was going to cry.

"That's the most movement I've seen him do for a long time." Dad sat down in his recliner and looked puzzled.

"See!" I hugged Dad. "He's coming out of his shell."

"I think you're right, Kendra. Maybe it's time we had Petey reassessed." Dad tried to touch Petey's head, but Petey moved and threw his leg up one more time.

"If he can do that, Dad, he can do more." I smiled a big smile. We had solid evidence that there was real hope for him.

"I'll make an appointment tomorrow for the regional center," Dad said, trying not to show emotion. "We'll see what Jackie Martins says."

Yes! I'd convinced Dad. It made my heart joyful, and it surprised me, because I hadn't felt that way in a long time.

Since Petey started his battements in class, he continued to do them every day that we went.

"There's something about the music, and the movement," I said to Jackie Martins, the caseworker, at the appointment. Unfortunately, I could tell that she didn't believe me. "I swear," I said. "Let me show you." I took Petey from Dad's lap in Ms. Martins's office and put his hand on the doorknob. I held onto Ms. Martins's bookcase and began battements. Petey watched me but didn't move. He grunted and looked around.

"Are you sure he did batons?"

"Battements," I corrected her. "And he did. He's confused. He's looking for the barre."

"A bar?"

"The ballet barre." I felt exasperated. I noticed that the cleaning crew had left a bucket and a broom in the corner, so I grabbed the broom and turned it sideways. "Barre, Petey." I showed my brother the plastic broom handle. "Ballet barre." I placed the broom between two chairs and I used the stick portion as a barre and did battements. Petey looked more closely, then walked over to inspect it. Then he slowly grabbed the broomstick atop the chairs and lifted his leg. But he stopped. He shook his head and grunted. He made a sign with his hand and touched his ear.

"What is it?" Dad asked.

"Music! He needs music," I said. "Do you have a radio?" Jackie Martins clicked a few keys on her computer.

"Classical?"

"Perfect," I stated.

Jackie Martins turned up the volume on the speaker, and the computer played a waltz by Strauss. I didn't know if Petey would respond to a waltz, but as soon as the music began, Petey threw his leg up into the air and raised his arm in a funny port de bras. "He's doing it!" I continued to do battements with Petey while Jackie Martins watched with amazement.

"That's incredible." She looked over at Dad. "He's responding." She then flipped through some files. "I think we can make the case for York School now," she said.

"Yes!" I jumped up and down like a little kid and smiled at Dad.

"My son, the ballet dancer," he said and shook his head.

⁂

The appointment was a success. Petey would now go to York, the better school. It was Friday and I couldn't wait to bring him to ballet on Monday again.

I worked with him all Friday night, playing all kinds

of music and showing him steps and moves. We twisted to jazzy music, and we threw our arms and legs up in the air to classical and country tunes. We ran through the recreation room to the living room, waving our arms to the music, then going down the entry hall.

As we passed the entry hall, I saw Petey's reflection in the hallway mirror. In the glass, I saw him coming out of his shell as he squinted his eye and ran past the mirror, and I saw myself there in the glass, helping him do it.

Petey ran back to find me and I chased him again, singing to the music. Petey loved it all. He scrunched his right eye up a few times, he ate better at mealtime, and he didn't fall asleep in that weird knocked-out way. At bedtime, he held his train toy and let me show him a picture book, and he actually stayed awake to finish it all. Then he fell asleep gently.

I went back to my room, forgetting all about my audition. I forgot about my illness, the medicines. I fell asleep from exhaustion, but it was a good tired. I felt like I'd done something that really mattered. I was helping my little brother discover the world around him.

❧

Saturday night came and I decided to wear a nice blue dress. It was short but still classy. I felt like a princess in it, and I wanted to be a princess like this each and every night. I dabbed on a little more mousse and brushed it through my hair, curled just enough to give it bounce.

"You look great," Dad said as I came down the stairs, dressed as if I was going to the prom.

"Thanks, Dad," I answered.

"Who is this rich kid again?"

"The editor of the *Seneca 'Zine* and"—I hesitated—"his father's on the Arts Council for Napa Valley." No sooner than I finished my sentence did Rafe knock at the door. When Dad opened it, his eyes went wide.

"You look amazing!" Rafe said, but I stopped dead. Rafe stood there in a black tux.

"You didn't say it was black tie," Dad said behind me in the entryway.

Horrified, I knew I made a huge faux pas. No, it was a disaster! I waited a beat, then looked into Rafe's eyes.

"I'll be right back," I said and grand jetéd up the stairs, leaving Rafe alone with Dad—a risky move.

Upstairs, I took my black ball gown off the hanger in the closet. I pulled at the blue dress, but the zipper got stuck, and I ripped the sleeve to get it off.

I threw the black ball gown on and recombed my hair, pulling out a few of the carefully ironed curls, along with a few strands of hair. I then inspected myself all over again in my full-length mirror.

I realized that I had hurt my leg a little, flying up the staircase like that, and it felt slightly numb, but I took a deep breath. Would Rafe think I was a total nerd? I should have realized that a debut would be black tie, but . . .

"You never mentioned it," I said, trying to save face, as Rafe and I left the house.

"It's okay," Rafe replied. "I got to see you in two gorgeous dresses." I laughed nervously, glad that Rafe was nice about it all, and that I didn't blow my entire night with a fashion catastrophe.

ॐ

The opera house was closed, but there was a door on the side that lit up in the darkness of the evening like a lone candle in the forest. There I was getting all fairy tale–like again. I admonished myself.

"It's a private concert room," Rafe said as he escorted me into the building. Rafe looked nice in his black tuxedo and somehow his black wire glasses became a better accessory with his tux than with his usual nerdy vest look. No, it was better than nice—he totally looked gorgeous.

The concert room was a small hall with its own little stage. As I looked around, I saw a cello propped up on stage beside a small chair. The audience buzzed with sophisticated chatter of "hello!" and "missed you" and "haven't seen you in a long time." Rafe directed me to a seat and handed me a program.

"Miss Ling Yu," I read the soloist's name.

"She's an up-and-comer," Rafe said as the lights dimmed for the concert to begin. I straightened up in my seat and arranged my dress for full ball gown effect. Rafe noticed and he smiled. A tingle of delight emanated from my heart as I heard the music start. It wasn't ballet music, but it was a performance, and performances were always exciting.

Rafe put his hand on mine, but it made me feel uncomfortable. It was too soon. The soloist walked out on stage, bowed after being announced, and then sat for a full minute before starting.

The music was beautiful and sad, then quick and joyful, and all the time the soloist's eyes were coy as she looked lovingly at her instrument. At times the music was a little slow. There was no ballet to go with it, so it seemed to be missing something. Rafe, though, tightened his grip on my hand and I felt like a princess. But I felt nothing for Rafe as the prince. He was nice, but I realized we had no romantic potential. Besides, romance and art did not mix in my ballet world. It really was just like in the movie *The Red Shoes.*

I loved that Napa Valley had more to offer than I thought. They did have cultural activities and guys who didn't mind going to them. Rafe squeezed my hand once more. Did Rafe feel more for me than I did for him? I suddenly felt worried, but then I thought about Troy and my heart fluttered. What did *that* mean?

At intermission, Rafe took me over to a drinks area where he ordered two ginger ales for us.

"You should remember not to wear the same dress twice." The voice made me turn and I saw a man. It was the white-haired man who was at the winery. The one who looked like . . . Rafe's father!

My heart almost stopped. It felt like a weather vane arrow had pierced my chest.

"That was uncalled for, Dad."

"This is your father?" I turned back toward Rafe.

"That was rude, Dad," Rafe defended me again, but then look confused. He turned to me. "Kendra, did you wear the same dress?" I thought I was going to faint from embarrassment, but stood my ground and said nothing.

"Just an observation." Rafe's father stood there in an expensive tux, which went well with his snow-white hair, perfectly groomed. He also wore the same wire glasses as his son. Rafe took my hand.

"This is Kendra." Rafe introduced me, and his father extended his hand. I didn't take it.

"I assumed so," he said, and looked away again. His indifference to the situation annoyed me even more than his rude comment. I could tell that he wasn't as nice as the refined black tie clothing he wore. Mr. Austin looked back again. "I hear you're a student at Manhattan Dance." I nodded. Rafe's father ordered a martini from the bar. From a full-length mirror on the opposite wall, I could see my princess sleeves and the beautiful cascade of the black, ball gown skirt. At that moment, I wished I were back in New York rather than suffering this humiliation. I could tell that Rafe's father didn't like me.

"I studied at Manhattan Dance for ten years, but then we moved to California."

"But she studies here in the meantime," Rafe interrupted.

"Why did you leave Manhattan Dance? Couldn't you have stayed?" Rafe's father took his martini from the bartender and looked me directly in the eyes. "They have a dorm."

"My dad got laid off." My voice grew a little quiet. "He . . . he took another job in the company out here."

"So, you couldn't afford to stay." The man's words were sharp, and I felt ashamed . . . Why was this man so rude? I wanted to run away like Cinderella, never to return, but I couldn't let this man get away with this. I loved Dad, and I knew that it wasn't his fault and it wasn't mine either. So I tightened my stomach, stood up as tall as I could.

"They're holding a spot for me at the audition in March," I retorted, not liking his snobbery.

"I see," he said, but I knew his words meant that I was some sort of a letdown and maybe not right for his son.

"She's going to be an apprentice, Dad," Rafe defended

me, but somehow I felt as if he was really trying to convince his father that I was good enough for him to date, and that he had also made the right choice. His father was not impressed.

I stood my ground.

"I used to see Alyssa Trent and Andrei Voltaskaya," I stated softly, "practice every day in class. It was just the normal routine." My voice was sophisticated and cool, but the anger inside of me was hot as *The Firebird* itself! My name-dropping made Mr. Austin turn quickly back to me. He seemed more interested again, but I didn't care. I had seen his ugly face of snobbery.

What if I also told him that I had MS? That I had a brother who was autistic? He and Rafe would drop like flies, I realized. I put my head up and looked Mr. Austin now directly in the eyes.

"Really?" Mr. Austin stared at me.

"Alyssa Trent emailed me yesterday," I lied. Mr. Austin looked a little guilty and I was glad. I wanted to wound him like he had wounded me and Dad.

During the second half of the concert, I had to fight back the tears that threatened to fall. Every time a tear blurred the image of the soloist onstage, I remembered my fouetté count and resolved to get back to New York as fast as humanly possible.

Chapter Fifteen

After that horrific night with Rafe, I realized that my prince and his father were nothing but nasty, shallow beings living on the artistic fringe. I, on the other hand, was participating in the art. What right did they have to be snobby when I did all the work? Actually, it was his father who was the real snob, but it might rub off on Rafe someday. Did I want to be with someone like that? It hurt, though. I really liked Rafe. But friends and boyfriends could always disappoint you.

On Monday I avoided the *Seneca 'Zine* after school and took Petey to the Academy of the Fields. I stood on pointe, center floor, then repeated the combination. All of my worries seemed to vanish when I danced, and I felt like the swan princess again, floating with ethereal arms, dancing on the hard, wooden floorboards.

It was the audition for the spring performance. The medicine must have been working well because I flowed like the dancer I hoped to become. I went into a series of fouettés and executed eleven of them perfectly, but faltered on the twelfth. *Just nerves*, I thought. My leg was sore from the injection earlier in the day. The new intramuscular shot hurt a lot because the new medicine burned going in. It was my third change of medication since the diagnosis.

I began another series of fouettés to beat my own record, and Becca, Troy, Mrs. Cassidy, and the other girls counted. ". . . nine, ten, eleven, twelve . . ." But I came down from the twelfth, out of breath. I grabbed a nearby towel and put it to my face and then around my neck.

"That's good enough . . . Melinda?" Mrs. Cassidy called the next audition, and the girl stepped out to repeat the same combination I had just finished. I was thankful that Bailey Adams dropped out of the running a while back. She'd laugh if she could see me falter.

I walked a few steps, then I truly did falter and had to sit down on the floor. Nobody noticed, luckily. I sat there for a moment beside Petey's old chair, but Petey was at the barre in the other corner, doing battements. Becca noticed my distress and came over. So did Troy.

"It's just a momentary lapse. I need my water bottle," I covered up, but Becca and Troy read me like a book.

"You need to rest," Becca said. I nodded, but when I moved my head, I felt dizzy.

"Oh no!" I felt the vertigo coming on. "Not now, please, I'm doing well." My voice was low, but it caught Mrs. Cassidy's attention.

"A spell?" She walked over to me and bent down. I

nodded. "You have to go home and rest," she told me. "I had a talk with the doctor and promised that I would not overwork you if you had symptoms."

Tears streamed down my face. It seemed like this was my usual situation for the last few months. In desperation, I imagined myself at the audition in New York, faltering; I also envisioned myself at Lincoln Center, plummeting to the stage beneath the lights, stumbling . . . falling . . . falling . . . Isn't that what a dying swan's supposed to do?

"Kendra!" Mrs. Cassidy's voice startled me back into reality. I shook off the negative thoughts

"I don't want to have symptoms," I said. "What if I have symptoms for the New York audition too?"

"You'll cross that road when you come to it," Mrs. Cassidy said, helping me up. "I'll get Petey," she offered, but I held her back.

"No. Let him practice for a moment." I stared at my little brother, who now bent down in a sweeping motion with his arm, obviously in imitation of us.

"He's getting better," Becca stated. I stared at Petey in disbelief.

"His motor coordination is improving while mine is deteriorating," I whispered.

⟶⟨⟩⟵

After going through another series of tests, I sat with Dad in the doctor's office. Petey wasn't with us; he was at York.

"We have one or two new treatments we can try."

"What about her future, Doctor? What are her chances to be able to dance in New York if she passes this audition in March?"

The doctor sighed. "She may do fine with medication for ten years, or she could deteriorate fast. The prognosis is still the same." Tears fell out of my eyes like a faucet that had just become unstuck. I couldn't believe the amount of water inside my head. Dad put his arm around me, and he sighed. I felt bad for him in the middle of my heartache. With his layoff and new job, he didn't need this too.

"Don't worry, Kendra. If you're up to it, I will fly you to New York, first class, for the audition." This should have cheered me up, but my heart sank lower. I felt a small bit of fight come up from my soul. I tried to dry my tears, but they didn't stop completely.

"What if I passed the audition and became an apprentice . . . and then I fell on stage? I'd lose my place in the company anyway."

"Possibly. They may not want to take you on with MS, no matter how well you do at the audition." Dad told the truth. I knew it.

"Well, it's up to you whether or not you tell them. But if they need a clean bill of health, I could tell them that you are fine on medication and should do well for now."

"But I couldn't lie to them." A single tear fell down my cheek. "I love Manhattan Dance too much for that."

"Well, the audition's in a month," Dad said. "Think about what you want to do." There was nothing else I could think about. It obliterated every other thought in my head. I looked out the window to hide my tears.

"What's the use?" I whispered.

❧

The relapse was temporary. I should have trusted the doctor. It came and went away just like he said it would.

Within a week, it was gone and my Spartan spirit returned. It was an odd disease, this MS. Most of the time I was okay, but I lived in constant fear of a relapse. You just never knew when it would hit you.

I was a Spartan warrior fighting against an inconsistent enemy. I felt the fight when I injected myself in the leg in the morning. I felt it when I pushed myself at practice or took a pill. I felt it when anxiety almost caused me to have a panic attack about my future at Manhattan Dance. But I continued on. Every day. Every single day.

Shaking my head, I deleted the doubt from my mind and threw myself into the rehearsals for the spring concert.

The Academy of the Fields ballet company would be only one segment of a multi-part program, a lot like the "Evening to Remember" show. Only this time, the local talent would take the stage at the opera house, which they offered free once a year to community performers.

Our entry was an excerpt from the ballet *Coppélia*. I got the leading role of the doll. Becca took it well. She got to play another doll in a smaller part and a townsperson in another. Troy played the part of Dr. Coppelius and enjoyed the masquerade with his beard, moustache, and white, powdered, scruffy hair. He made us laugh constantly as we rehearsed in ballet class.

"I'm Dr. Coppelius and you are under my spell." Troy came up from behind like a villain and scared me constantly in class. He did it again, and I screamed. Troy, dressed in folk costume, looked too hysterical. With his aged makeup, he was more like Pinocchio's father than the Seneca High track star turned Svengali.

I posed as the doll, Coppélia, with my exaggerated

makeup and ringlet curls, while Troy circled me and did some turns. My arm came up mechanically and I accidentally hit Troy in the face, and we broke into another round of hysterical laughter.

We went back to practicing, but as soon as Mrs. Cassidy walked out of the room to answer a phone call, Troy grabbed me by the waist and wouldn't let go.

"What are you doing?" I asked, but he didn't reply. The others in the room practiced their parts individually, so they didn't notice. "Let go," I joked, but he didn't budge.

My eyes then caught our reflections in the mirror. In the ballet room glass, I could see Troy looking down at me as if he was in love; I don't think he was acting. I stared at the reflections and watched as Troy's hand softly touched my face. As he lifted my face up toward his, my eyes left the mirror and focused on his eyes gazing intensely into mine. He still said nothing.

I looked deeply into his eyes, which stared back down at me in such a gentle yet powerful way. He didn't want to let me go. It was obvious. It almost seemed as if he would kiss me at any moment and his face drew very near.

I held my breath, bracing for the kiss, but Mrs. Cassidy came back into the room, and Troy straightened up and spun me around, and we continued on with the rehearsal.

I felt all a-jitter, fluttered, from the almost kiss, the spin. I was dizzy, but it wasn't the MS this time. It was Troy. I felt a second flutter in my heart, and I thought about Troy a little differently after that.

During our practice, Mrs. Cassidy asked me if Petey could be a soldier in the show.

"He could do his battements, with his wooden-like movements," she said.

"That's a great idea," I said, but Dad said, "Definitely not! He might get scared onstage."

◦ℰ◦

The night of the performance, I peeked outside the heavy, red, velvet curtain from the right side of the stage. There was Dad, and also Petey, dressed in his little maroon suit, in the second row. I also noticed Rafe and his father sitting a few rows behind them. The sight of them made my heart feel like a hummingbird inside my chest. They would get to see me dance. Maybe it would make Rafe's father feel guilty.

What if I faltered? Would they laugh at me? Would the MS be the culprit, or would it just be nerves? Most important of all—would I doubt myself?

"Places!" the stage manager called, and several groups ran about backstage. There was the Folkloric Hispanico, with their colorful, full skirts of yellow, orange, blue, and red. Behind them were the "Teen Tappers," whose director told them to keep the taps quiet. On the other side of the wings, I could see the jazz group, in sparkles, and a classical music group with their stringed instruments.

"Kendra!" Mrs. Cassidy's voice now called out. "There you are!" She and Becca came up to me.

"I'm nervous," I admitted.

"Me too." Becca shivered. "I think I'm getting a cold back here." She sneezed, and Mrs. Cassidy handed her a tissue. "Maybe it's consumption, like the girls in the classic novels . . ."

"You're not dying of consumption. You'll be fine."

Mrs. Cassidy wiped a smear of lipstick near my mouth. "Don't touch your face!"

"I really am nervous," I admitted.

"This will be your test for New York," Mrs. Cassidy said. "You can do it." She left to attend to someone else, and I went farther backstage, passing a mirror. My makeup looked good. Mrs. Cassidy painted a doll face on me with red circles on my cheeks, and she outlined my eyebrows with a wide arch. My doll costume with its folk skirt made me look like another person altogether. *Shine!* I told myself.

My shyness would not emerge now. I was somebody else.

"Kendra!" Troy called out. I saw our group, dressed as dolls and townspeople, squeezing behind the Ballet Folkloric. All of them were trying not to step on one another's toes or smash each other's costumes. Inevitably some did step on toes and smash costumes. Little squabbles broke out and Mrs. Cassidy and the Folkloric director had to calm everyone down.

The lights dimmed in the audience. The jazz group was already positioned for the opening number.

As I waited in the wings, Mrs. Cassidy brought the little wardrobe closet on wheels for me to climb inside. She said, "Good luck," and closed me in, shutting the two little doors, ready to wheel me out. Coppélia didn't arrive this way in the real ballet, but it worked for our shorter recital version.

Inside, I wondered what Rafe and his father would think of my performance, and whether I'd feel dizzy or numb or nervous or . . . I didn't have time to wonder more. I could feel the wheeled wardrobe move as it was put into place in the center of the stage. I breathed so hard that

I thought Petey and Dad and Rafe and his father could hear me.

The Coppélia music began, and Troy and the others danced around the wardrobe, jumping and pounding the wooden stage. It was dark and stuffy inside the wardrobe, and I almost sneezed too, but I held it in. As I heard my entrance music, my breath stopped. I prepared and got into character. Troy opened the cabinet and carried me out, and I held my arms and legs stiff like the doll I was supposed to be. Troy set me down center stage and I began mechanically, then broke into a series of ballet moves, slow with arabesque, then into a series of fouettés that people later told me brought loud applause.

It was all a blur. I didn't remember all of my performance. I never heard the clapping. All I knew was that we lined up for the bows at the end of our piece, and I got to do three curtsies in professional ballet poses.

On the way out of the opera house, Rafe approached with this father, but I hurried away to Dad's car before they could reach me. I didn't falter, I felt great, and I didn't want anything like Rafe or his father to ruin it.

We had victory pizza afterward in the Cassidys' roomy farm kitchen, and Mrs. Cassidy praised the professionalism of the show.

"What about us? We did the work!" Becca, Troy, and I all talked at once.

"Not bad . . . ," Dad said seriously, then laughed. "You were all excellent."

Petey shook his head as well and held Mrs. Cassidy's glass of apple juice with two hands as if it was meant for him. He had already taken a sip, as evidenced by the little bit of spit on the rim of the glass. He looked like a little gentleman in his little maroon suit.

"Milk for you, young man," Mrs. Cassidy said as she replaced the apple juice glass in his hand with a glass of milk.

"My name is Peterrrrrr."

"What?" We were shocked.

"Peterrrrrr," he repeated, then shook his head again and scrunched up his right eye.

I stared at my brother in disbelief.

"Petey! I mean, Peter!" I jumped up and hugged him. Dad followed me, and we all crowded around Peter and smiled at the miracle boy who sat in a kitchen chair with a glass of milk and a sly wink.

❧

Later that night, I couldn't sleep. I was too wound up from the performance. The music of *Coppélia* played in my head, which spun with the dance and the lights and wardrobe cabinet and Petey sipping Mrs. Cassidy's juice and talking.

I was excited that Petey finally spoke. I knew he could do it! It was the music and the movement. I was right. It made me feel great to know that I made a difference with him. If I made a difference with him, then maybe I could make a difference with the rest of his classmates too. I decided to volunteer at Petey's new school. Petey was going to be okay. I mean, Peter was going to be okay. Laughing, I felt happier than I had in months.

I also felt proud that I hadn't faltered in the performance, and that I passed the test Mrs. Cassidy set up for me. The real test was to come at Manhattan Dance's audition class.

If I did well there, I'd become an apprentice member of the Manhattan Dance Company.

Doubt crept into my mind. What if the MS kicked up in a relapse? What if I fell on the floor of the ballet class in New York or onstage? Most of the time, I knew I'd be fine, but it could happen. What were the odds of faltering when I was in top form? No! I wouldn't allow it. That was the MS talking. It was the nature of the disease. Fine one minute, and down the next. But I'd be horrified if my leg gave way when I was so close that I could practically touch the apprenticeship! I'd be humiliated beyond belief. I'd feel like an invalid in the midst of elite performers. "No!" My mind couldn't think straight anymore, and panic closed in on me like a monster. I began to hyperventilate and felt like an addict in withdrawal, writhing in bed from anxiety, until a thought flashed through my brain.

The image was blurry but familiar, with little flames in the background. The strong odor of burning candles wafted into my nose. A calm feeling came over me as I remembered my mom and me in church. I was about six, but I remembered the sight of the large, white pulpit where a man stood and talked to everyone. I remembered the pretty stained-glass windows with Crayola colors that let the sunlight shine through them. And I remembered my mom smiling at me as we sat in the pew and said a little prayer together from a small book. A prayer . . .

"Dear God." I folded my hands and looked up at the ceiling from my bed. "I haven't been in a church since I was ten, since Mom died, but . . ." A feeling of serenity ran through me as I whispered the words. It made me want to continue. "I haven't been to church for a long time." I closed my eyes to make my prayer more earnest. "I hope you haven't forgotten me, God. If you're still there, would you help me?" I clasped my hands together more tightly. "I want to get into the ballet company . . ." But, no, that wasn't right. I had to start again. "God, I can't ask you for something selfish, like ballet, when kids like Petey need help, but could you help me know what to do? Should I dance or . . ." I could hardly finish my sentence. ". . . or should I find something else to do?"

What else could I do if I didn't dance? I thought about Petey and his friends at the autism school. I thought about my article for the *'Zine*. I thought about Manhattan Dance without me. "God, I know you have the answer. Please, please, tell me . . . tell me what to do." I unfolded my hands and the calmness engulfed my entire being. "Thanks for letting me talk to you again. I think I'll do it more often now." I let out a huge sigh, rolled over, and then fell into a deep, serene sleep.

In the middle of the night I woke up laughing, because I dreamed that I danced *Coppélia* in my black ball gown and that Rafe and his father complained that I wore it a third time. Then for some reason, Rafe's father wore Troy's Dr. Coppelius outfit, beard and all, and when I woke, I realized that Rafe's father was acting like a Svengali to Rafe, pulling the strings and controlling him, too, like a puppet.

"Weird dream," I said and fell back to sleep.

The weirdness continued throughout the next day.

Bailey, the head cheerleader, was actually nice to people. She obviously didn't feel well, so she didn't have the energy to act like a harpy or whisper like an evil spirit down the school hallways.

Then I saw Sylvan, who sat with the drama club at lunch. She seemed to be enjoying it too as she talked with the other students about *Guys and Dolls,* the school musical. She even joined in singing "Lady Luck" while her goth table friends looked on, perplexed. The weirdness continued, though, even after I got home from school.

The rain that had threatened to fall all day came down just as I stepped inside the house.

"Wow!" Dad stared out the door. "We're in for a drenching."

"I thought it never rained in California," I said as I took off my jacket.

"The rains come in the winter here. I just heard it on the news." Dad closed the door. "Gonna be a doozy."

"Is that Chinese food?" I followed the aroma, which permeated the house, and spotted the traditional white boxes on the table in the kitchen. "But you hate Chinese food."

"I passed a Chinese place on my way to get some deli sandwiches for dinner and thought you'd like this better," Dad said. "Glad I went out before this deluge." Dad put some plates on the table. "I know you missed your favorite takeout in New York." My stomach growled when I took in the aroma of the Kung Pao chicken, Mongolian beef, and pork fried rice.

"Thanks, Dad." I squeezed him in a big bear hug, and then checked the time on my cell phone. If I gobbled the food down quickly, I had time to eat and still get to the Academy of the Fields for class.

The rain outside hit the window like a shower of hard, icy crystals, and I looked outside to make sure it wasn't hail. It wasn't, but it sure looked threatening out there. A flash of lightning appeared and a roll of thunder roared.

"I guess you'll stay home today with the rain," Dad said and bit into his sandwich.

I scooped out a huge helping of Chinese, despite my diet.

"No, I'll go. Can't miss class."

"They'll probably cancel it."

"No, they won't. Besides, the audition's in a month."

"And you want to be in good shape for the audition, so no driving. Besides, it'll give you a night off to rest or decide what you want to do about the . . . well, you know . . ."

"You can say it, Dad. The MS." Dad put his head down. He didn't know what to say. "I'll make my decision about the audition class soon." Dad perked up again.

"Maybe we can all play a board game with Petey tonight or make cookies with him." I looked over at Petey and he squinted his right eye, and it made me smile back at him.

As I ate the Chinese food, I thought about Dad's words. I wanted to audition to get into the company. I didn't want to audition. I hated pro and con decisions. You never knew if you were going to make the wrong choice. What if I could dance? What if I couldn't? It tore my heart out all over again. I was so indecisive, even though I had success with *Coppélia*.

"Rain's dying down a bit." Dad noticed. That was my cue to bolt. I ran to the hall, grabbing my dance bag.

"Petey?" My voice rang out in the house. I heard his little feet scurry from the kitchen. He was ready for ballet.

"No. You can't take him." Dad walked into the room and grabbed Petey by the hand.

"Why not?"

"It's storming out there." Dad pointed to the window. "Besides, I just heard on the news that minors can't drive with children in a car for a year. It's too dangerous. No more Petey! Take a break from ballet. It's too dangerous to drive anyway." I began to protest. Dad pushed me back gently. "The roads are slippery."

"So?"

"Remember, you're a new driver. Don't take any more chances like you took on that long, long drive. You never did tell me where you went that night. And, by the way, if your tires ever hit an oil slick in the rain and the car spins, you turn into the spin, not against it."

"Don't worry. I'll be careful."

"Despite opinions to the contrary, you're still a new driver." I grabbed Petey's other hand but Dad pulled him back. Poor Petey was in the middle of a tug-of-war. "No," Dad said. What was up? I didn't understand this new reaction.

"You know me. I'll be careful." Dad's face registered a stern no. "You just don't want Petey to do ballet—"

"That's not it." Dad coughed. "I mean, that is it, a little. You can't drive him anymore. DMV rules! I missed that, I guess." Dad led Petey to the kitchen and turned back to me. "Don't use Petey as a crutch anyway. Stand on your own, Kendra."

"Crutch? You think I'm using him as a crutch?" I exhaled a large breath in disbelief. "I'm helping Petey. He's improving!"

"That's true, but in helping Petey, you're neglecting your own life. You have a lot to think about. And I don't want you to be too dependent on each other. Sometimes you have to separate."

"Is that what the doctor says?" I snapped back, but I felt bad as soon as I said it. Dad looked at me with earnest eyes. He meant well; I could see it.

"No more Petey," he said. Petey looked back too. He reached out to me, then put his hand up in a ballet arm movement.

"Pete . ." I stopped as Dad gave me a look. Dad took Petey's hand more firmly.

"Come on, boy. Wanna make train cookies?" Dad and Petey left the room.

I felt abandoned as Dad took Petey away. I'd gotten used to him sitting in his chair, doing battements at the barre. All of the dancers liked him too. It made me feel unsure without him. I plopped down on a living room chair near the entry hall, bundled up in my jacket.

Petey needs me, I thought, but I realized that I needed him just as much. I didn't know why, but somehow he steadied me. My leg felt numb again, and I slapped it.

"Stop it! " I shouted. The MS continued to creep up my leg and it grabbed my calf muscles in a grip of steel. The multiple sclerosis took control of my body like a creature inside my legs, and there was absolutely nothing I could do about it.

What good was all this medicine I had to take anyway? I just wanted to scream at the MS. "Go away!" I yelled at the unprotected myelin inside of me. Dad came running back with cookie dough all over his hands.

"Is anything wrong?" I didn't answer. I was still shaking

from the thought of going to ballet without Petey, shaking from all the events of the past few months.

"Don't drive," he said and walked away again. I heard Petey grunt from the kitchen.

A crutch! My own little brother? It was laughable. Wasn't it? Was he a crutch? The shaking stopped and an eerie calm swept over me. Did I use Petey to keep my mind off of the MS? Feeling more vulnerable now than ever and wondering if the MS would permit me to ever dance at all, I panicked.

"Forget the rain," I said and grabbed my dance bag and left—alone.

❧

The road was slippery and very wet. It was treacherous to drive through, but nothing would stop me from getting to ballet class, not even the MS. I was on a mission to get back to Manhattan Dance.

Dad was right, though. It was stormy outside. Feeling glad that I left Petey home in these terrible conditions, I steered carefully with windshield wipers zipping back and forth like scissors cutting across the foggy glass. I drove almost two miles down Chapel Street, not far from the Academy of the Fields. It was dangerous but the slippery roads presented no real problem. I splashed through puddles, hoping I didn't flood my brakes, and heard the slosh, slosh of the water beneath my tires as I rode along. Then, suddenly, the world became a huge blur.

The scenery around me became a hazy mix of gray fog, water, distorted farmhouses, and headlights. Not knowing what to do, I screamed inside the Honda. As the car whirled around, I realized that my tires lost traction. I'd hit an oil slick. Right away I panicked and turned against the spin, and it spun harder. Then I remembered Dad's words. I turned into the spin and the car stopped.

Stunned, I sat frozen, shaking, staring at the rainy world around me, wishing that Dad wasn't right all the time. It was a scary spin, but I actually survived it. Luckily, I had the road all to myself. I guess everyone else had the sense to stay home.

I put my head down on the steering wheel, wondering why my car decided to go into a mechanical chassé turn. I felt so alone. My heart beat rapidly as the car chug-chugged its motor, mocking me, as if to say, *"You're not mature enough to drive a heavy piece of machinery."* The chug-chugging of the motor droned on and on, and it made me shudder. I saw the fog of exhaust rising from the bottom of the car, and the encroaching dusk that threw a purple haze of dimming sunset over the wet landscape ahead.

I got my perspective back and realized that the car was sideways on the road. Readjusting the wheel, I righted the car.

Should I go home? Keep going? I then saw the Academy of the Fields sign down the road, despite the rain that hit my windshield harder and harder. I followed the ballet school's sign by squinting like Petey, trying to see between the fog and the rain. The occasional street lamp and my car headlights steered me like a lighthouse until I reached the warmth of the Cassidys' house.

❧

The lights were out in the ballet school, so I knocked on the side door of the house. The rain came pouring down on me, but I could see the light inside. It was so inviting, like a fireplace on a sparkly Christmas card. Becca answered the door.

"Mom!" Becca turned back to me. I was dripping wet from the rain. "What are you doing here? Didn't you get my text?" I shook my head no as I entered the warm kitchen. Mrs. Cassidy came to take my coat.

"Kendra, I'm glad you're so dedicated, but you risked an accident coming here in the rain." Becca took my coat from Mrs. Cassidy and hung it up.

"And you could get pneumonia!" Mrs. Cassidy looked around outside for my brother.

"No, I didn't bring Petey with me." I didn't want to tell her that I almost did.

"Well, you'll have to stay the night. I'm not risking you driving back home in this storm. I'll have to call your Dad."

"He'll be so mad." Mrs. Cassidy looked at me. "He told me not to drive . . ."

"And you didn't listen." I shook my head and sat down at the kitchen table. Mrs. Cassidy called Dad from her house phone.

"Kendra!" Troy walked into the kitchen in sweatpants, without a shirt. "What are you doing here?"

"Put a shirt on. We've got a guest for the night." Mrs. Cassidy pushed Troy back out of the kitchen, holding the phone. "And we'll have to get you something to sleep in too . . . Mr. Sutton!" Turning, Mrs. Cassidy waved to her daughter. "Becca . . ."

"I'll take care of it as soon as I finish clearing the table."

"I'll help," I said. Becca smiled and handed me a dish towel to dry off some of the pots as Mrs. Cassidy talked to Dad on the phone. "I notice that Troy doesn't have kitchen duty."

"That's because I'm a guy." Becca and I both laughed as Troy came back into the kitchen wearing a sweatshirt with large superheroes on it.

"Hey, it's old, okay?" We could hardly clean up. "Mom didn't do the wash yet, and it's all I have to wear."

"Oh," I said. "Superheroes don't do laundry either?" Troy sat down at the table.

"Olympian gods don't work," he said and smiled.

"Oh, yes, he does," Becca countered. "He's off today. We *all* do dishes and laundry. Today it's my day, tomorrow it's Mom's again, and the next day is Troy's."

"And I do a better job too!" Troy grabbed a small bottle of orange juice from the fridge and offered one to me, which I didn't take. "You girls and your diets." He laughed and gulped the drink down almost all at once.

"We're going to be famous ballerinas," Becca stated. "And you're going to end up fat."

"Who's fat?" Troy stood up and flexed his muscle. "Toned. That's what it is—toned." Troy did look toned. In fact, he looked really good. Troy then smiled at me and his eyes softened. "I'm glad you're here, Kendra." He smiled again, and his mythical persona faded, and genuineness came forth. I liked this Troy, the genuine one. I stared into his eyes too, until . . .

"Out! Cretin!" Becca pushed Troy out of the kitchen.

Troy popped his head back in. "We'll watch a movie later."

"Out!" Becca ordered, then laughed. "We *do* have a lot of movies," she said.

⁘

Later in the living room, Mrs. Cassidy brought us all hot chocolates. The dangerous drive in the rain now seemed so worth it, sitting here in the Cassidys' living room. Becca gave me her pink sweat suit to wear for pajamas, and I felt cozy and warm again. The three of us nestled into the large sofa and went through a pile of film choices saved on the TV's DVR.

"What kind of movie do you want tonight?" Troy asked.

"We don't have to go through the genres again, do we?" I groaned.

"Sure we do. Tonight's horror movie night."

"No!" Becca and I screamed, and Troy laughed heartily.

"Just kidding. What about a romantic comedy?" Troy looked at me, and his eyes were intense but gentle at the same time. I tried to figure out how that could be true, but Mrs. Cassidy interrupted us and held up a DVD.

"What is it?" we shouted.

"You'll see," Mrs. Cassidy said and popped it in player. "Something from my generation," she said. "Enjoy!" She also set a box of tissues down on the table in front of us. We all looked at her, puzzled, as she coyly said, "Good night."

Sitting for over two hours, we laughed and cried as the romantic movie suddenly turned really sad. We actually cried a lot. *Buckets* would not be too cliché a word for how much we cared. As we watched, huddled together in the center of the sofa, sniffling and feeling every emotion under the sun, Troy put his hand on top of mine, but his eyes never left the screen. I felt warmth go through my system as I stared down at his hand. I don't even think he knew he did it. In fact, if he had known, I think it would have embarrassed him. He was totally oblivious.

Later, Troy removed his hand from the top of mine, right at the saddest part of the film. I stared at his face, which was full of emotion, in a guy sort of way. At that moment, I wondered what it would be like if Troy actually did turn his head and kiss me. Then I shook myself out of the daydream. Why would I think that?

Forcing my attention back to the television, I saw that the girl in the movie was very ill. Was Troy thinking about me? Feeling sorry for me because of the MS? Is that why he touched my hand? Did he think I was going to die too? Was I going to die? Fear swept through my heart. Would it be possible that Troy really cared for me, the way the guy in the movie cared for the girl?

My thoughts drifted back to the movie as it ended. The credits came up and we were all destroyed. A small tear still hung in Troy's eye, and I tilted my head a little, trying to figure out this guy who was really made of mush underneath.

Chapter Sixteen

Four days later, it was sunny again, and after a chastising from Dad about the drive in the rain, I was back at the Academy of the Fields. I was grounded, but it was worth it for Troy to touch my hand like that. Still, I couldn't get the anxiety of the March audition out of my mind. I felt off, like an actor who forgets his lines right before going onstage. Would I flub my moves? Would anxiety throw me off at Manhattan Dance? The worry affected my barre work, which was unspectacular, and the center floor work, which was uninspired. I danced badly, all because I was getting nervous about New York.

"Feeling sorry for yourself?" Mrs. Cassidy walked by and inspected my développé.

"No." I extended my leg in à la seconde. "Of course not."

"Then work!" Mrs. Cassidy demanded in my ear. "Perfect

those extensions." I tried the extension again and held the pointe but faltered. My heart was not in it.

I had had a relapse again over the weekend, and even though it was a small one, it was enough to make me lose confidence. I then heard Mrs. Cassidy call for the diagonal, and the girls lined up for pique turns. As the girls turned one by one across the floor, I entered the line, but my mind was on my MS, not on spotting. I did the turns double time, bumping into the girl in front of me, and tripping another.

"What's the use?" I walked away from center floor and grabbed my towel. "I'll never get into the company." My Spartan attitude eluded me. I didn't know what was wrong.

"Outside!" Mrs. Cassidy pointed and led me to her office. The tiny office barely fit the two of us, but she stood authoritatively, took me by the shoulders, and looked directly into my eyes. "You did well in *Coppélia*. Why do you doubt yourself again?"

"I don't know." I felt shaky emotionally. I had been strong, but the other night, when Troy put his hand on mine, I went into jelly-leg mode again. It was Troy's fault. Or maybe it was the movie's fault. Both sucked the strength right out of me because I allowed myself to lose focus.

The trouble was that I liked being close to Troy. But I couldn't tell that to Mrs. Cassidy, and I knew that emotion of any kind with Troy would have to wait until after the audition.

"I think I'm just nervous," I responded. "It's just an off day."

"You have a choice," Mrs. Cassidy said. "You can let the disease destroy you, or you can stand up and fight to achieve." She became really serious. "You might not ever get signed by a major company because of the multiple sclerosis. You'll have to face that possibility. But there is the possibility that you could get a contract. You could also dance with a smaller company closer to home." Shocked, I pulled away.

"I'm going to dance with Manhattan Dance!" I yelled it out.

"You could teach."

"I want to dance!"

"I know that, Kendra." Mrs. Cassidy held me at arm's length. "I left dancing to teach, because I wanted girls to learn ballet the right way. I saw so many girls with overdeveloped muscles and bad form from bad teachers, because they learned incorrectly."

"But you were so good. You stopped performing!" Tears streamed down my face. "You had it in the palm of your hand, and you gave it up. How could you do that?"

"There is value in teaching and serving others, Kendra. It's rewarding. It takes a special gift to train good dancers, and I wanted to be that person."

"But I haven't even started my career. I need to be . . . with Manhattan Dance."

"You and a million other girls." Mrs. Cassidy gave me an understanding smile.

My heart raced, my breathing went into hyper mode. I felt crazed. Ballet was my whole life, my existence. "I have to do it, Mrs. Cassidy. I'm going to New York for the audition, and I'm going to make it! Do you believe that I can?" I noticed that the girls from class hung around the doorjamb nearby to listen, upset. Mrs. Cassidy waved them away.

"I don't know, Kendra. Maybe Manhattan Dance will take you. I really can't predict what they'll do. The question is . . . what do you want to do?"

My voice became very quiet. My illusions were shattering faster than glass breaking on a polished marble floor.

"I want to be known . . ." I looked up at Mrs. Cassidy. ". . . for my grand fouettés, my graceful adagio, beautiful arabesque, dramatic port de bras, and my soft, tiny, rapid bourrées across the stage that make me look like I am floating above the floor." Lost in the elusive vision, I continued, "That's what I want. And I know I can do it." I looked into Mrs. Cassidy's eyes, waiting . . . waiting for an answer that would solve the problem for me. "What would you do if you were me?" I stared straight at her. Mrs. Cassidy sighed and sat down at her desk.

"I danced and had a good career, Kendra, and I was lucky to have my health. But I can't tell you what to do. It's something that you have to sort out by yourself."

"But . . ."

"You know what's right and what's wrong. If I tell you to do it, and it's the wrong decision, you'll regret it. If I tell you not to do it, and you could have been successful, you'll hate me. I don't want you to hate me, Kendra. You must make this decision by yourself."

"But how?" Mrs. Cassidy patted my arm, like a mother.

"A dancer has to dance through fatigue, sickness, and emotional turmoil. No matter what else is going on in her life, she must find the mettle to get up on that stage and perform. A ballerina has to be strong, Kendra, not only physically, but mentally. Endurance is the key. It will give you strength for all that you do in life. There is a special strength to ballerinas. You must always remember that."

"I know." My voice was quiet again.

"You have some thinking to do, young lady." Mrs. Cassidy put her arm around me more tightly.

I gulped, hating that the decision I'd now make would affect my entire future.

"Why did I get this disease, Mrs. Cassidy?"

"I don't know. But it's how you deal with it that makes you a champion."

"You told me that before. I guess I didn't listen."

"Try to find the answer in here." Mrs. Cassidy touched her own heart. She cupped my chin affectionately and returned to class.

❧

My thinking lasted over a week. I thought about the audition from the time I got up, staring at my pink mobile on the ceiling, until the time I finished my homework and went to bed at night. My thoughts were obsessed with the decision. I wrote those horrid pro-and-con lists to try to sort it out as Mrs. Cassidy said, but I came up empty. All I had was a bunch of lists that changed every time I wrote them, with pros winning one day and cons winning the next. It was a stalemate.

I *did* decide, however, to quit the 'Zine. It was too hard to see Rafe Austin, who was such a fringe-art snob. He seemed nice but wasn't. Troy, on the other hand, seemed obnoxious, but he wasn't. Appearances could be deceptive, like those mirrors that reflected my body image every day in ballet class. On the outside, I looked like an aspiring dancer, but on the inside, I was sick. The mirror showed only a part of me, just like I saw only a part of Rafe and Troy.

Losing myself in the school library, I sat at a table with a stack of books that made me look like a Rhodes scholar. Despite the appearances, I found it hard to write, so I just stared straight ahead until I laid my head down on the stack of books and fell asleep from stress.

"What's the matter?" It was Sylvan's voice. She sat down at the library table across from me. I was silent for a moment, debating how much to tell her.

"What will I do if I can't do ballet?" I asked. Sylvan looked perplexed. It was understandable—she didn't know about the multiple sclerosis.

"You can do a lot of things."

"Like what?"

"Anything you want," Sylvan said.

"But ballet is who I am." I looked at Sylvan carefully. The flower in her hair was now purple, and it matched the lavender eye shadow, which was less vivid today than usual. "It's like you said."

"Is ballet all that you are?" Sylvan's words startled me. "People are like diamonds," she continued. "They have many facets that can shine." Sylvan then got up from the table and grabbed a book from the library shelf. "Is ballet really all that you are?" She then left with her goth friends, but after she left, her words stayed with me all day long.

It was funny. Sylvan only showed up when I needed her most of all.

⁂

After school, I walked to forget the madness inside my head. I walked down the suburban streets with wine names.

I kicked a soccer ball back to a group of younger girls. But the ball went much too high for them, soaring over a fence into someone's back yard, and they were mad. I quickly walked on. Clearly I didn't know my own strength or the level of my own anger.

The regional center found a nice new aide for Petey who could watch him in the afternoon, and she shuttled him back and forth to York. His emerging speech got him accepted, but his absence at ballet left me empty, as if a part of me was missing.

"The aide can stay with him now," Dad had said.

"No," I protested. "Petey's responding to the music at ballet. It's a new therapy for him. He must go."

"You have too much responsibility," Dad responded. "He's a special-needs child. Leave him home. Have some fun."

Dad dropped Petey off to ballet a few times after that, and Petey responded. Troy touched Petey's head and the weird thing is that Petey didn't flinch or move away. He let Troy ruffle his hair, and he scrunched his eye. My little brother, who didn't understand the world, knew exactly what he wanted. If only I did.

My walks became more frequent now. I told myself that I was cross training, but the truth was that I was still thinking, thinking, and driving myself crazy in the process. I'd walk a few miles sometimes and not even realize it, then have to circle back again before it got dark. I wanted to walk until I could see into my soul and search for answers.

A few days later, after the school bus dropped me off, I went for another short hike around Apple Glen. I'd planned a short walk, but again, my thoughts took over.

I was on autopilot and didn't even remember going by familiar stores and street signs.

I began to hum, thinking about the lyrics. It was a song from my father's era, the one I heard that night on that awful drive home from the cliff. My soul felt as though there was a war going on inside me. Sadness overwhelmed me, interspersed by bursts of artistic passion.

I exploded into sobs as I walked by a small wood. I cried for an eternity, or so it seemed. Stopping to regain control over myself, I noticed that there was no one nearby, so it was easy to cover my crying, which began to subside. All of my perseverance, sadness, struggling . . . I just had to get it out. The song was true. Was I going to let my dream dissolve into thin air, or was I going to continue to fight?

As I lifted my head to face the rest of the day, I noticed that there was a church ahead of me on a tree-lined street. Its white steeple was impressive and its well-manicured grounds called out to me somehow. Yes, say a prayer. I needed one now.

I walked up to the building and stared. Something made me go up the five steps to the entrance, and something made me open the large metal-and-wood door. I entered before I could think any more about it.

Inside, I saw how large the church really was, almost like a cathedral or something. The pulpit and altar were very grand and made of marble, almost like the one my mom and I used to see. Walking on tiptoe, I went down the center aisle and watched several other people praying by themselves. I wondered what they were praying about, and if they had major life decisions to make like me.

I slipped into a pew and quietly sat down, deciding to

say my prayer. We weren't really churchgoers, I realized. Dad stopped taking us when Mom died. He didn't "have the heart," he said, to go anymore. But now I looked all around me. It was strange being here, since I hadn't been in a church since I was ten.

I looked up at the candles that were lit and I stared at the interior architecture, with the stained glass windows so large and colorful, like the ones I remembered. I saw the holy glass people looking back down at me. It was oddly comforting.

I prayed a little childish prayer I learned from my mom, but couldn't remember any more, so I said the same one three times, hoping that my repetition would send my earnestness up to God, who would find a way to solve my problem. But I then felt guilty. I knew there were starving children in Africa and wars around the world. Like I'd told God before, there were families who were homeless, people like my Dad who got laid off but still couldn't find a job like he did. There were people with real disabilities, like being blind or lame . . .

"You've been sitting here an awfully long time." The voice behind me made me jump. I didn't speak, but turned around to spot a pastor, who walked up to me. His white collar stuck out from under his shirt. I remained silent. "Wanna talk about it?"

A tear fell from my eye.

"I'm a dancer, and I have multiple sclerosis." I blurted out my story in all its drama to the pastor. I could tell he felt truly saddened by the situation, but he put on a wise face. He sat down in the pew ahead of me and turned back to face me.

"You've been given an opportunity."

"Opport—?"

"I know it doesn't seem like it, but yes. You can decide if ballet is truly your life's calling or if it's something else."

"What else could it be? It's my whole life!"

"Now, isn't there anything else that ever interested you?" the pastor asked. I thoughtfully sat for a moment and remembered Sylvan's words the day before.

"I kind of like science, writing . . . but ballet is tunnel vision, you know?"

"All the arts are," the pastor replied. "Music, painting, acting . . . it takes tunnel vision to get to the top. I understand that. But there are so many other things for you to explore in this world that I know you'd enjoy. You're young." The pastor smiled and waved his hand with a flourish. "Your life journey is all ahead of you. It's just beginning." The pastor then chuckled. "My life journey, however, is shorter, and I have to deal daily with that fact." The pastor looked me in the eyes, and I felt that he was sincere. "You have the ability to shape your life, and those of others by your actions."

"I guess you're right." I looked down at the marble floor. "I just don't know what to do."

"God will reveal it to you when he's ready, and when you're open enough to receive it."

"I guess I never really thought about it before. Ballet is my life." I looked down, thinking. "Ballet *was* my life." I looked back up at the pastor.

"Sometimes God changes our life plan, but he always has a reason, you know." The pastor paused when he saw that I wasn't buying it. "Oh, we might not see or even understand the life plan he gives us. We can only see the piece of it we're standing on now, like a cobblestone. We hop from one cobblestone to another, not being able to see the entire blueprint of the road. That's why we sometimes get so mad at God, but in the end, he's always right, you know."

"Maybe," I said, "but I really want to do ballet." I wiped my nose with an old napkin from my purse.

"Then do it. Dance!"

"But what if I fail?"

"Didn't anyone at that Manhattan Dance Company ever fall or make a mistake?"

I smiled and even laughed a little to myself as I remembered Andrei Voltaskaya and his wicked fall.

"I just thought I'd have to be perfect, and the MS makes me imperfect."

"And that's what makes a great dancer," the pastor pointed out. "All those quirks that make people different. You want to stand out, don't you?"

"Of course."

"Do it," the pastor said, "if you want to, but find something else if you can't. Remember that you do have options."

"It's funny. I never thought I had another option before." The pastor smiled again, then got up to attend to an old lady in a pew, who was crying near the altar. He looked back and waved. I lingered to reflect on his words just a moment more, and Sylvan's words as well. I left the church, vowing to come back for services again very soon.

⁂

It was late winter, and the March days in California were warm. Some of the trees still had no early leaves, but the palm trees always had their large fronds, so it looked not much different from winter or fall or summer. The breeze, though, was still cool, and it whispered in the air.

I got into my car with my dance bag and drove off in the eternally sunny weather. I entered the Academy of the Fields and walked up to Mrs. Cassidy, who sat in her little office doing paperwork.

"Tax time," she said and shook her head.

"I've decided to go for it." Mrs. Cassidy seemed surprised as she looked up from her paperwork. "I'm going to the audition."

"Okay," Mrs. Cassidy said.

"I don't know if I'm ready, but if I don't try now, I may never have another chance. Who knows what'll happen in a year."

"You could become part of the ensemble, get a featured part, or play Giselle . . ."

I did a double take. "Giselle? Me? But you said they wouldn't take me . . ."

"Stranger things have happened. At any rate, I'm proud of you, Kendra. I didn't mean to be so harsh the other day."

"No, you were truthful. But I'm going to try anyway."

"At least you've made a decision." Mrs. Cassidy stood up. "Whatever you do, Kendra, always remember the strength of ballerinas."

"I will." I looked at her and smiled. Becca and Troy must have heard me as well, because they quietly walked into the office and smiled at me too.

❦

On the plane to New York, I had my earphones on to watch a movie, but my mind was on my fouetté count. Dad was back in Napa Valley with Petey, but he'd arranged for a driver to take me to the dorm at Manhattan Dance. I'd stay there tonight, do the audition in the morning, and then wait while they made their decision. If they took me, I'd stay in the dorm as an apprentice. If not, I'd leave on a plane the next day.

How would I feel when I saw Miss Irina again? She broke my heart, not just from ignoring my request to live with her, but also from ignoring me completely. Would it affect my technique in class? I couldn't let it. The apprentice program was too important. Besides, if I got into the apprentice program, I wouldn't have to see Miss Irina anymore. Mr. Anders was the head. I sighed with relief.

And how would Liz react when she saw me? It was clear that she'd dropped me as a friend in favor of Sara. She hadn't emailed me in months.

When I'd left New York, it was my home. Now, without the bond of Miss Irina and Liz, it almost seemed like a strange place. *I'd have to overcome that obstacle too*, I thought, *just like I had to overcome my illness and go on*. My eyes closed in thought, and I dozed off.

A few hours later, I walked from the plane to the terminal. I saw a lot of drivers holding signs. I almost panicked being by myself. Which one was my driver? I glanced around and saw a driver holding a sign with my name on it. The sign made me smile.

As I sat in the nice, black car, I watched the John F. Kennedy Airport fade away in the distance, and I looked at everything out the window to take it all in. I had seen it all before, but now I saw it with new Californian eyes.

It felt kind of funny to be without Dad and Petey. What if I did become an apprentice at Manhattan Dance? Would I really live by myself in New York City? Would I do well on my own with my father and brother three thousand miles away? Suddenly, I didn't feel confident anymore. It was a big city. I knew it well, but being here alone was a different story. I couldn't visit my old apartment on West 79th Street. My home would be a new home in New York—the dorm. Would I be able to do it?

I thought back to my bus rides in the morning on the way to Madison School for Girls. I remembered all the interesting people and stores I used to see. As we drove off the West Side Highway into mid-Manhattan, I saw the steam rise from a manhole cover, and I noticed unique shops on every corner and the pizza places and business people and tourists that crowded on the streets. I saw the yellow cabs again, driving on top of one another and somehow never crashing together. A cab honked right in front of a sign that read, "No Honking, $250 fine!" Despite my nervousness, it made me laugh.

I couldn't stop thinking that I was on the east coast, and Dad and Petey were on the west coast. In California, they made the wine that they drank here in New York. The connection made me feel better, and I smiled to myself.

Yep, I was in New York again. Sitting back in the seat, I took out my cell phone and texted Dad that I was in Manhattan. He texted back that I should call him when I got into the ballet dorm, and I promised I would.

❧

"Kendra!" One of the girls from my old class recognized me and waved. "You back?"

"We'll see," I responded and waved in return. I looked around the dorm lobby just as the housemother came over to greet me.

"I'm Mrs. Burkov," she said. "I think I remember you."

"I used to visit friends here," I answered. Mrs. Burkov had me sign in on the log and took me to my room. We walked down the hall and I saw girls talking, some stretching their legs against the walls.

"No shoe marks on the walls," Mrs. Burkov admonished them, and their legs came down again. "Go to the practice rooms," she said, and they walked off in a slump. I saw a demi-soloist go by.

"Here's the key. Breakfast is at seven." She smiled, then said, "Welcome. Good luck," and I thanked her. Physically I felt good, but mentally I really needed the luck.

I felt excited to see the girls in the dorm hallway. Memories of visiting Liz here flew through my mind, but that was when we were friends. I wondered if Liz still had the same two roommates, the sisters. I guessed it didn't really matter anymore. Did it?

As the key opened the door, I saw that I was all by myself. There would be no roommates tonight. I was grateful and threw my roll-on bag on the floor, sat on the lower rung of the bunk bed, and clicked on the TV with the remote.

Swan Lake music emanated from my cell phone. It was a text from Becca.

"Good luck!"

The text made me smile. I texted back a "Thanks" and threw myself back on the bed to watch TV and relax after the long plane ride.

The *Swan Lake* music played once again. At first I thought it was Dad, but then I remembered I'd changed his ringtone to play Herr Drosselmeyer's music from *The Nutcracker*. This time the text came from Troy.

> If they don't take you, Kendra,
> they're out of their minds.
> Do your fouettés until you drop!
> I miss you already, Coppélia. <3

"Oh, Troy," I whispered. These words were more than just friendship. They had to be more. My heart fluttered a bit. This was more than a twinge, it had to be.

I felt like I did on that rainy night at the Cassidys' when we watched that romantic movie and Troy touched my hand.

No! Not right before my audition! I had to be focused. Instead of being upset, though, I started laughing.

I knew that I had good friends, the true-blue kind, and ones who would never forget me when I was on the other side of the country. Well, one of them was a friend, anyway. The other . . . well, maybe something else—a real boyfriend. I smiled once more and looked around the small dorm room again.

"If I got into the company, this could be my room," I whispered. I walked around the room with its TV and tiny bathroom, dresser, table, and lamp, and window that faced a brick wall with a small view of the street below, if you turned your head just right.

There was also a mirror on the dresser. I gazed into it and saw my thin reflection. Mirrors were my life, at least that's what I used to think. Funny. They only reflected the outside. There was so much more to people than that. Mirrors didn't reflect what was on the inside. I wondered why I hadn't realized that until now. I stared for a moment more at the too-thin girl in the mirror who had gone through so much to get back to this point. Me.

Chapter Seventeen

The next morning I walked into my old Manhattan Dance training room, the room where Andrei Voltaskaya and Alyssa Trent practiced every day. Neither of them was there. In fact, no one was there yet.

I was already wearing my black leotard and pink tights, so I sat on the floor and put on my pointe shoes. I put my dance bag down on the floor in front of the mirror, where all the other bags would shortly join it. Taking my time, I looked at the peach walls with white molding. I gazed at the wooden floor and looked at the large wooden windows that let New York City's light shine through.

My nose picked up the scent and dust of the resin, and I could see the resin's powdery residue in the corner where it sat in a little wooden box, and it made me smile. How often had I dipped my pointe shoes in there?

I touched the wooden ballet barre and felt its light, grainy texture, smooth from all the years of sweat and wear. There was the piano that the Julliard music student played for our class, waiting for its musician to arrive. I saw the mirror that reflected my dancing every day of my life in New York. It all brought me back to that last day, that day when I was so upset, when I did a so-so grande jeté and Liz called Miss Irina a witch.

My heart didn't sink as I had expected when those memories came flooding back.

That surprised me, though it was just as well. I had my audition to think about, and I didn't need any distractions. I was nervous enough already.

And Miss Irina . . . How would I feel when I saw her? She never answered my email. Dad was right. She didn't care. It hurt me a lot.

I pushed it all out of my mind. I had to be that Spartan warrior now.

Endure!

Resist!

Achieve!

I wasn't going to let all that had happened in these last six months stop me from achieving my goal. I wasn't going to let the MS rule my life. I was going to dance a perfect class. I needed to pass the audition, to prove to myself that I could.

There was a rustling behind me as girls came into the room one by one for class, and they recognized me immediately.

"Kendra!" They crowded around me, and I wanted to cry, this time with tears of joy. They took turns hugging me. "We heard you were back. Are you back for good?"

"I don't know," I said but smiled anyway. I waved to another nice Russian teacher who walked past the ballet room, but then watched as Liz walked in with Sara Harrington and went straight to the barre. Liz had seen me but put her head down as if she hadn't.

"Oh, Liz," I whispered. It tore at my heart again how friends could be friends one minute, then not be friends the next.

Just then, Miss Irina came into the room with two others of the dance staff. I stared at her and froze. Miss Irina's heavily lashed eyes slowly looked up and we locked eyes. I gazed at Miss Irina, and she stared right back. She lowered her eyes and looked to the side, away from me. Then she clapped for class to begin, and the girls fidgeted with nervousness.

"Judgment come from Etienne Anders, Director of Apprentice Program, and Aleksandr Minskov, Director of Company." Etienne Anders had been a Russian ballet star. He'd shortened his name from Andreyev to Americanize it, but we all knew that Etienne Anders was *the* person to decide our fates, because he was from the Kirov. Aleksandr Minskov we rarely saw, since he was more of the money person behind the company, but he was still an accomplished dancer in his own right.

All of us applauded in honor of the two judges.

"At my country, we have no time for school, just dance," Miss Irina continued. "You have plate of cake here in America, but I wish luck to do well." Miss Irina looked over at the assessors and they nodded. "At the barre!" The girls all scurried to find a highly visible place and some squabbled over the placement, but Miss Irina settled it quickly.

I went into battle mode and grabbed the barre.

"Plié, first, soutenu . . . brush, brush . . ." I did good extensions and pushed even harder to be better. The assessment went on for another twenty minutes at the barre.

"Center," Miss Irina stated, and I saw the two judges taking copious notes about us in their notebooks. I dipped my foot into the resin box and moved to center floor.

"Combination . . ." Miss Irina's voice faded and I went into muscle memory. I aced the first combination and waited for the second. It was a much more difficult round.

Maintain lift, stretch the jump, land like a feather. I had it ingrained in my brain. I couldn't judge my own performance, because I concentrated on every move, every hand and finger placement, every transition in time with the music. "Piqué, piqué, grand jeté, pas de bourrée . . . close fifth, tendu . . . effacé . . . développé, attitude, promenade, hold, close fifth, croisé, glissade, ensemble, cabriole, coupé, pas de bourrée, fourth, triple pirouette, close . . . preparation. Fouetté. Begin count. And . . . one . . . two . . . three . . ."

Miss Irina's words floated in and out. All I could hear was the wind whipping around me as I went round in the spin. ". . . ten . . . eleven . . ." I threw my leg to create the force to whip me around. "Fifteen, sixteen . . ." Several girls dropped out. "Twenty, twenty-one . . ." Several more fell out. "Twenty-two . . ." I held steady. *Endure! Resist! Achieve!*

There were only three of us left, and then Sara Harrington dropped out. I saw her from the side of my eye. Liz stayed with me, though, like she always did. Now it was only the two of us, like old times, head to head.

"Twenty-four . . . twenty-five . . ." Liz dropped out. ". . . Twenty-six, twenty-seven, twenty-eight . . ." I finally came down, and though out of breath, I ended with a controlled pose.

I think the other girls applauded, but I wasn't sure. I was so happy that my multiple sclerosis hadn't kicked in. The medicine did its job this time, and I didn't feel dizzy once. A smile went across my face.

The MS, the move to California, Miss Irina and Liz— they had not defeated me. Suddenly, I felt a little weak and needed my water bottle. I grabbed it from my bag and drank about half of it right there in the ballet room. Was it the dizziness returning? Exhaustion?

I wanted to drop to the floor from exhaustion, but I had to keep it professional. The two assessors watched us even after the class ended. How did we look? Were we thin enough? Willowy enough? Flexibility? Strength? Did we have star quality?

"Give us fifteen minutes to confer," Mr. Anders said, and Miss Irina nodded.

"The assessors to be grade your work," she said to us, and then oddly, she looked back over at me and looked away again. "Into my office. You will know in fifteen minutes."

We all left the room, but as I passed Miss Irina so closely that I could touch her, she spoke, but not to me. She looked at Sara Harrington and touched her shoulder.

"Very goot, Sara. My prize pupil." Miss Irina flashed her eyes at me. "Well, you made it, obviously."

"We'll see," I said. I broke the gaze, and left to escape.

I then felt a twinge go directly through my heart. It's

like that when someone you loved betrays you. The hurt turned to anger. It was mean. Miss Irina switched prized pupils faster than someone switched toothpaste brands. I did more fouettés than any other student in that assessment . . . More than Sara. Why, even Liz did more than Sara Harrington! I had never realized how cold a person could be until that very moment.

Outside Miss Irina's office, the girls crowded around, talking excitedly, moaning about missed moves, and boasting about exquisite ones. I stood with them for a few minutes but then walked away.

"Where you going?" a girl asked. She was new. I didn't recognize her. "The results will be here any second." She jumped up and down.

"To the restroom," I said. "All this excitement, you know . . ." I lied, and the girl accepted my explanation. I walked away. Liz never even noticed.

❧

Outside the building, I looked up at the New York skyscrapers, then over at Central Park. I walked inside the entrance to the park and found my old gazebo seat, where the green trees bordered the large lake, where I used to feed the ducks, and where I'd laugh at the little frogs who'd stick their noses out of the water. There were no frogs in the water today, and the lake was still.

Oddly, the green of the trees and bushes and the smell of the grass and the dirt reminded me of the vineyards of California. I broke out crying on the gazebo seat because of the pressure of the audition, the meanness of Miss Irina, and the joy that I felt knowing I did a good job, despite it all.

As I sat there in the sun of a cool March day, I thought hard about my journey.

I'd come back to New York and had achieved my goal. I did well in the class and had the best fouetté count. I breathed in the New York air and smiled a smile bigger than I had in a long time.

Whether or not they offered me the workshop to vie for the role of apprentice didn't really matter now. Miss Irina didn't matter now. I proved to myself, despite the multiple sclerosis, that I could dance. I had to fight twice as hard, but I did it.

If only Manhattan Dance knew that.

What would I do if they offered me the apprenticeship? A wondrous feeling of freedom came over me. I squealed out loud with joy. A sigh of relief came out of my soul, so big that my heart tingled. It was as if all of the events of the past six months came down in that single moment, and my being was relieved of all its burdens. I knew that I had done well, and it was a fabulous feeling.

They wouldn't know, I reasoned. Did I really have to tell them about the MS? What if I fell onstage? At Lincoln Center? I reconsidered it. Embarrassed in front of hundreds of people?

The medication would work, I countered myself.

Could I get away with it? Would it be so wrong to hide it, sign the contract, and hope that the MS wouldn't kick in? I knew at that moment that I wanted it now more than ever. I did well, didn't I? I wanted it so much—*Giselle, Swan Lake*, the lights, the roses, the white blur of tulle . . . I wanted it all.

Deep in my heart, I also knew at that moment that I

could not accept an apprenticeship. I loved Manhattan Dance too much for that. I could be selfish and take it, but if I faltered during a performance because of the disease, it wouldn't be fair to the company. And I wouldn't be a professional.

I stared out at the water of the greenish lake in Central Park and discovered how hurtful it was sometimes to be mature. As I watched a squirrel run up a nearby tree, I remembered that even though my dream was fading away, I did have a backup plan.

I made the decision right there at the edge of the lake that I was going home—home to California, that is. I'd continue my ballet training with Mrs. Cassidy at the Academy of the Fields and prepare for the summer program in Los Angeles. Los Angeles was closer to home, the ballet company was excellent, and I could monitor my illness better there. Maybe I'd even try that support group Dad told me about. There'd be teens there who knew exactly what I was going through.

And I'd been thinking about Petey's school for some time too. I decided to go to school myself to get my BA, ballet or not, to work with special-needs kids through dance therapy. And I just might take journalism as a minor, in case I got the itch to win another award for my sharp investigative reporting.

I smiled to myself as I thanked God for helping me to make this hard decision that would affect the rest of my life.

Yes, I would teach autistic children through dance therapy. God had revealed my calling, and it was a great feeling to finally know that.

"Thank you, God. And thanks, Sylvan," I said aloud. Ballet was who I was, but it wasn't all of what I was. She was right too.

And the MS? Well, I would take it one day at a time and thank God for every moment that I felt well. Life would go on, and so would I.

I was going home . . . where my family lived, and where a great guy named Troy also waited for me.

Wouldn't Dad be surprised?

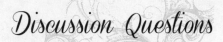

Discussion Questions

1. Did you ever want to become a ballerina? Why? Was it the art, the fame, the tutus, or something else?

2. Have you ever encountered an obstacle? How did you deal with it?

3. Coping with a family member who has a disorder can be stressful, especially when it is a sibling. Would you have had as much patience as Kendra did with Petey?

4. To be perfect in your art, you must be devoted. Many girls play musical instruments, do gymnastics, or figure skate. What do you do, and how much time do you devote to your activity?

5. Kendra moves from New York City to the vineyards of Napa Valley, California. Which location would you prefer to live in, and why? Back it up with good reasons.

6. Kendra receives a diagnosis of multiple sclerosis, which affects her life plan. How does Kendra react? Would you have reacted in the same way?

7. Many students have to switch high schools due to a move. Kendra loves her old school in New York but has to readjust to a much larger coed high school in California. What are some problems of attending a new school?

8. Kendra has to sort out which friends are "true blue," and which ones are false. How do you uncover that truth?

9. Kendra disregards her Dad and drives to Big Sur without permission. Sometimes teens have to make decisions for themselves, but when is it okay to do that, and when is it not okay?

10. Kendra knows that she has to be ethical at the end of the story. Have you ever had an ethical dilemma and had to really think about what to do? Give an example.

11. Rafe and Troy are both interested in Kendra in the novel, but which one was the best choice for her? Why?